Jitters

Chris Harmon

To my Mom, Chloe,
and those who stuck with me

CONTENTS

THE UNWANTED GUEST

Grace and Justin Knotz watched the movie silently. In the film, Alice ran in the woods, holding a baseball bat in her hand. She came into a clearing in the woods. As the darkness and the trees surrounded her, her big brown eyes bulged in fear. She was drenched in perspiration. Her straight brown hair blew in the wind. From behind, she could hear his pounding footsteps fast approaching. Crazy Eyes was coming.

He was going to kill her next. Alice ran from the clearing and into the trees, hands trembling, almost causing her to drop the bat. She sprinted viciously, her sneakers pounded on the ground. Then, in the middle of the woods, she stopped. Alice breathed heavily, trying to catch her breath. She wasn't exactly in the best shape.

"I gotta get out of here," Alice muttered, "I think I'm losing him."

Oh, but she was wrong. From behind, she heard stomping footsteps fast approaching. Before she could run away or move or do anything, Crazy Eyes emerged from the shadows. He was about eight feet tall, almost as tall as the trees. His abnormally large height made Alice's surroundings even darker. She could only see his unusual eyes, one orange, and one red. Peculiar for a human. They glowed like high beams. Moonlight reflected off his dirty face as he bent down and stared at Alice.

"Ya wanna die, Alice?" he asked. Crazy Eyes lumbered closer and held up a large dagger. His eyes were so blazing, Alice shielded away from the brightness. Crazy Eyes pressed the blade against her face. "I'm gonna slice you up."

"No!" Alice yelled.

Crazy Eyes' smile faded and turned into an evil grimace. Alice had to act fast, or else she was going to die. Instantly, Alice swung the baseball bat and hit him in the stomach.

"Ooh," Crazy Eyes uttered as he fell to the ground. He had his hand over his stomach. "Shit."

Alice began hitting and hitting Crazy Eyes with the baseball bat in the face repeatedly. Blood trickled from his nose. CLICK.

"Hey!" Justin Knotz cried. "Why'd you do that?"

"I told you two, no more horror movies," Mrs. Knotz said as she ejected the CD out of the DVD player.

"But we were at the best part," Justin pouted as he tore his jet-black hair. He gave Mrs. Knotz a dirty look.

"No more, like I said," Mrs. Knotz put the movie back on top of the stack of horror movies underneath the TV. Then, she walked briskly out of the room. She turned back around and said, "If I catch you two again, you're going to be in serious trouble."

"Fine, take them. You caught us. It won't happen again." Grace Knotz said. Mrs. Knotz disappeared down the hallway.

"Ugh, she took away *Killer in the Woods*," Justin groaned. *Killer in the Woods* was the kids' favorite horror movie. A man broke into a cabin in the woods and killed a group of defenseless teenagers. Grace and Justin had seen it over a hundred times. Their parents banned them from watching horror movies in the house. They were angry about this news. At least, Justin was. It happened two days ago.

"Horror movies are rubbish," Mrs. Knotz had said when they were eating breakfast one day.

"They're rotting your minds," Mr. Knotz added.

"But they help us become well-adjusted human beings when we get older. They'll make us stronger and more self-aware. That's what my friend told me.," Justin protested. Grace didn't say anything. She just ate her breakfast.

Our parents still have the most power over us. We can't do anything about it, Justin. Just give it up. Give all of it up. Grace thought.

But their parents ignored Justin's argument and went back to eating.

Their parents still kept the horror movies in the guest bedroom for some reason. The kids couldn't live without those horror movies and missed a lot of new ones that came out. Grace started to scan through the other stack of DVDs under the TV. They were all boring and lame.

"How are we supposed to live without them," Justin asked. Justin grabbed the TV remote and threw it across the room in frustration. It hit the wall so hard that a crack formed in it.

Oh no. Justin is angry. I can't stand to see him like this. Things always got terrible when he was angry. Two summers ago, She and Justin, along with their parents, went to the amusement park. Justin ended up having a meltdown because he wasn't tall enough to ride on a big roller coaster.

He was mad for the entire day. He refused to speak to his family. After that, they got ice cream, and Justin dropped his cone. He was furious that he tackled some random middle-aged lady in the ice cream line. Park security had to come and get him off of her. The whole family was banned from the amusement park after that. That was two years ago when he was twelve. Now, Justin was fourteen, and his anger issues were growing worse. Their parents always paid most attention to him, while Grace barely got any of their attention.

"J-j-Justin, p-please calm down." Grace stuttered as she put her hands over her face, trying to protect it. She knew that the punches were coming. Her brown eyes began to water.

"I'm not gonna calm down! I'm fucking livid right now!" Justin shouted as he broke from her grip. He cracked his knuckles, and his face grew tomato red. Justin began to make weird grunting noises. In one sudden motion, he slapped Grace in the face.

"Ow! Stop! Please!"

Justin slapped her again, harder this time.

"S-stop, y-you're hurting...m-me," Grace said. She dropped herself to the ground and burst into tears.

"Bitch.," Justin muttered.

Mr. and Mrs. Knotz stormed into the room with concerned expressions. "What's going on in here?" Mrs. Knotz asked. She saw Grace on the floor, crying. "Grace, what's the matter?"

Grace lifted her head up. She saw Justin mouth to her, "You better not tell."

"Umm...err...I," she whimpered.

"There's a bruise on your face. Go downstairs and put some ice on it." Grace stood and walked out of the room. Mr. and Mrs and Knotz followed her out of the room and went separate ways. She went to the kitchen and took a block of ice out of the freezer.

Grace knew that she had to listen to Justin. If she tattled on him... well... she would've been in a body bag. Grace adjusted her pink beanie over her short brown hair. She needed a beanie on all the time, even indoors. One time, Justin had cut out a couple strands of her hair. This scared

Grace so much that she always wore a stylish beanie at all times. She went back upstairs to the guest bedroom, where Justin sat on the bed.

"Why...did...you slap me?" Grace quivered.

"Cause, you deserved it."

"J-Justin—"

"Well, Why'd Mom have to fucking ban the thing we love?"

"D-d-don't worry, w-w-we'll finish the movie."

"When?" Justin growled; his brown eyes were ablaze in anger.

"Uh..er...soon." That was all Grace could say. She didn't know when. She also didn't realize that they would soon be in a horror movie of their own. Grace went back to her room. She had a neatly made queen-sized bed and bedside table with a pink lamp and alarm clock. She had a desk with another lamp in the corner of the room. There was another desk area with a vanity mirror where she did her hair. She looked in it to check out the new damage Justin inflicted. Her mother was right. There was a big pink bruise on her face. She still had the scab on her bottom lip from when he scratched her with his long fingernails one time.

Grace started crying. She put her hands in her face and continued to wail. She couldn't show or tell her parents or anyone about her scars. That's why she had to wear long sleeves. Other people thought she was a klutz. She was a punching bag. Still crying, Grace got up from the desk and laid down on the carpet.

* * *

A few hours later, Justin and Grace were downstairs, watching television. Grace flipped through the channels to see what was on. Their parents came downstairs, elegantly attired. Mrs. Knotz muted the TV.

"Your father and I are about to go out on our first date in forever," she said, smiling and clutching her purse. "Grace is in charge,"

"How come she gets to be in charge?"

"She's more mature than you," Mr. Knotz said, narrowing his eyes at him.

"But how come--"

Mr. Knotz held up a fist which made Justin shut up. He gulped loudly and stared at the TV.

"Carl, we have to get going. Our reservations are at nine." Mrs. Knotz pushed him towards the door. "See ya kids, don't burn down the house." They hurried out the front door. Grace looked out the window as the car sped out of the driveway onto the street.

"Are they gone," Justin asked.

She nodded.

"I'm gonna get the horror movies," Justin sprinted upstairs and returned minutes later.

"Let's watch *Nightmare Troubles*," Grace said, grabbing it from the top of the stack.

"Wait, let's finish *Killer in the Woods*," Justin insisted. He took that movie from the stack. Quickly, Grace shoved *Nightmare Troubles* into the DVD player.

"Move out the fucking way," Justin grunted. He tried to shove Grace away from the CD player, but she resisted.

"Stop, you're hurting me!" Grace shouted. Justin snatched the DVD out of Grace's hand and pushed her to the floor. He towered over Grace, red-faced. Tears were falling down his face, and his fists were clenched. Justin bared his teeth, revealing his shiny pearly whites. He cracked his knuckles.

"I'm telling Mom that you pushed me, you stupid fat fuck!" he sobbed. "I fucking hate you! I hate you so fuckin much!"

"C-c-calm d-d-down Justin. "Grace pleaded, "Please, we can—" They were interrupted by a frantic knock on the door. Both kids stood still, staring at the wooden door, surprised that someone was there.

It can't be Mom and Dad. They would use their key to get in. Grace thought. Their parents always told them that if someone was at the door... don't answer it. *But what if it could be someone we know? Grandma? Aunt Beatrice? Who?* She thought. They could be visiting. The loud knocks continued, breaking through Grace's thoughts.

Quietly, She tiptoed up to the door and looked through the peephole. Grace gasped at who she saw. It was not one of their family members but a tall man.

"Open up," the man rasped, "I brought the package," he announced as if he were talking to someone inside. It was hard to tell whether the man was young or old. He had a young face with near-perfect skin with just a few blackheads. Yet his voice sounded old. The man could've been twenty or seventy. The man had pea-green eyes that seemed so... angry. As if he wanted to harm whoever was inside.

A shiver of fear swept over Grace, making her not open the door. She felt something wasn't right. The man continued to bang on the door harder than before.

"Who is it?" Justin asked.

"It's a man,"

Justin looked through the peephole.

"There's no one fucking there,"

"What?" Grace shoved Justin away from the peephole. Sure enough, the man was gone. "He must know our parents," Grace concluded. The man had to have left when he realized no one had answered the door. She and Justin went back to the living room and sat down on the couch. Grace was about to turn on the movie when they heard a loud crash coming from the kitchen.

The kids jumped up from the couch in surprise. He was breaking into the house—ready to kill them. In a panic, the kids ran upstairs into Grace's bedroom. Justin slammed the door shut. There were no locks on any of the bedroom doors. Grace pressed up against the door.

Call the damn cops," she instructed.

Justin grabbed her phone and began to dial frantically. Grace could hear hard footsteps going back and forth from the kitchen to the living room from downstairs. She heard kitchen items fall on the floor, the furniture being moved, and the sound of glass breaking. Tears ran down Grace's cheeks. They were going to die young. She knew he was going to come up and kill them.

"Police said, thirty minutes," Justin said breathlessly. They sat there for a couple more minutes but all was quiet downstairs now. Grace could hear a pin drop down there.

Where is he? Why hasn't he come to kill us? Grace had to know where he was. Quietly, she opened the door a smidge and peered out into the hallway. She heard heavy footsteps running up the stairs; when she saw the man come up the stairs, Grace let out a choked cry. The man moved around the hall, breathing heavily.

"Please don't see me. Please don't," Grace whispered to herself.

Finally, the man sprinted down the hall to her parent's bedroom and slung the door open. He went inside and left the door slightly ajar. Grace shut the door and stuck her back inside the room to report, "He's in Mom and Dad's room."

"Out the window," Justin whispered, pointing across the room.

Grace narrowed his eyes at him. "That won't work. What if we break an ankle or something?"

"No, we won't! Let's just do what I say!"

"Shhhh. He'll hear you."

"I don't care! I hope he kills you! I'm going out the window!"

Grace couldn't take it anymore. Thoughts clouded into her head, interrupting what Justin was screaming about. *Out the window… What a terrible idea…too high up. We'll break our ankles, and by the time the police arrive, the man would've already killed us. Justin is crazy. Enough of him. Tired of him pushing me around. I'm taking charge.*

What could they do, though? They were just teens. Then, something hit her like a tidal wave. A swell of realization, *Psycho Killer*. The girl defended herself against a man who was trying to kill her. Grace knew what to do. Like the girl in the movie, like the people in all of the horror movies they watched. They needed to kill that man.

"J-Justin, we have to *kill* him," Grace said.

"Are you crazy? What if he has a gun or a knife or something? We'll never kill him."

"Going out the window isn't gonna work. This is our only choice. We've watched plenty of horror movies. The main leads always survive because they defend themselves. We have to do that!"

"But we're gonna die. We have no weapons!"

"We gotta find some. There has to be some in this room."

Justin stared at her for the longest time. "Yeah, let's do it," he finally agreed.

"Awesome."

Quickly, they began to search the room for something to use to defend themselves. "We could use the lamps," said Justin. He held up Grace's bedside table and desk lamps. Grace grabbed the desk lamp.

"We gotta be quiet," she whispered. Slowly, they walked into the hallway. Grace saw their parents' bedroom was left wide open. The room was ransacked. She heard soft, shuffling noises and noticed the light was on in Justin's room. It was trashed. His mattress on the floor, clothes everywhere, his books thrown off of his bookshelf, and broken school certificates had been knocked off of his wall. The thief smashed Justin's piggy bank, and all of the coins and dollar bills fell to the floor. He bent down to pick up the money with his back to Grace and Justin.

At that moment, Grace started to get second thoughts. *What if this doesn't work? What if he is armed and has a gun or a knife or something? This is such a stupid idea.* She inhaled softly and then exhaled.

We can do this. If we die, we die. It's over.

"Come on," Grace whispered. Quietly, they tiptoed into the room, holding their lamps in a batter's position. Two inches behind the man, they struck the lamps at his head. Surprisingly, the man didn't get knocked out—he spun around.

Dazed, he stared at them. The lamps didn't seem to hurt him. The man's eyes began to focus on Justin's. The man lurched at him, but Justin gave the man a hard quick kick in the stomach.

"Ooof," the man mumbled as he put his hands around his stomach. Then, he started to charge at Grace.

"Grace, watch out!" The man tackled her to the floor. He put his hands around her neck. She let out choked gasps.

"H-h-helpppp," Justin started to pull the man off of her, but he struggled. The man clenched his hands tighter around Grace's throat, causing her to turn purple. She knew that she was about to die. No air left.

"Get off of her! Get off! Get off!" Justin screamed. He stood there watching the man choke Grace.

"You're mine now," the man whispered to Grace as he kneeled down on the floor. She started thrashing and kicking her legs. She thrashed and thrashed with all of her strength. The man's grip loosened his grip on her throat as he tried to use his free hand to grab her legs. Grace struggled to get to her feet and unexpectedly fell backward, somehow elbowing the man in his nose and neck. Choking and bleeding, he turned over on his stomach. The man lost his balance and fell flat on his back. During his struggle, he managed to grab the desk lamp. He charged Justin, holding the lamp above his head.

"Look out, Justin," Grace said hoarsely, pointing. Justin tried to duck, but he was too slow. The man had struck the lamp at his head, causing a big bruise on the side of Justin's face. Then, the man dashed out of the room.

"Why... didn't you help me," Grace croaked. Justin stood in the corner of the room, rubbing his swollen bruise.

"I'm so sorry, I'm just...too scared,"

"You c-can't be. W-we have to—"

"I know,"

"Come on," They chased him. He ran into Grace's bedroom. Quickly, the stumbling man grabbed the chair to Grace's desk and heaved it unsuccessfully toward them. Grace scampered at the man and threw herself on top of him, knocking him further off balance.

She pinned him to the floor.

"Get off me, you stupid girl," The man kept thrashing his arms and legs wildly. He kept making soft wailing sounds. Justin stood at the doorway. His big brown eyes were wide, and he was drenched in perspiration. He managed to punch her in the face, but Justin had hit her much harder than that. "Justin, help me!" Grace cried.

"I-I can't. I'm too s-scared."

"Do something!"

"Uhhh…" Justin scanned around the room, and his eyes stopped on Grace's pillows on her bed. Justin grabbed one and threw it to Grace. "Grace, smother him. He's pinned down." She grabbed the pillow and pushed it on the man's face. Grace held her hand tight on the pillow. The man was swinging his arms and legs wildly. He made soft mumbles and cries.

"Mmmmmmm! Mmmmmmm! Mmmmmmm!" The man muffled through the pillow.

"Help me," Grace uttered. Justin ran to his sister and pushed the pillow on the man's face with as much force as he could muster. They pushed the pillow harder… Harder… harder until the man's arms and legs jolted to a stop. They no longer heard the muffles or felt the resistance. All was quiet in the room… So quiet.

"Is he dead?" Grace asked as she backed up. Cautiously, Justin removed the pillow from the man's face. His eyes were closed, his mouth was gapped, and the blood from his nose was staunched.

"I, uh, I don't uh think he's breathing," Justin reported.

They wrapped themselves in a big hug and cried.

"We did it,"

They hugged for a few more minutes and then let go. "What do we do now?" Justin asked, wiping tears from his eyes. Grace pointed to the phone.

"Call Mom and Dad," She handed Justin the phone, and he began to dial...

* * *

The police and the ambulance came a short while later to retrieve the burglar. Their parents came eventually after.

"Oh my god! My babies!" Mrs. Knotz wrapped her children up in a hug. "Are you guys okay?"

"We're fine," Justin said. He unwrapped the hug. Mrs. Knotz's crying had smeared her makeup.

A police officer came out of the house. He had black hair and brown eyes.

"You're brave young people. You did what you had to do. I'm glad you're safe." he said.

"Scary," Grace whispered.

"The man strangled me and bruised her neck." Justin showed the officer her bruises. "He hit me with a lamp."

"You guys need to go to the emergency room," The officer said.

The first-responders came out of the house, carrying the man on a stretcher. They put him in the back of the truck.

"I'm glad you kids are okay," The officer said.

"We'll heal," Justin said. The EMTs brought Grace and Justin on their truck and drove them to the emergency room. Mr. and Mrs. Knotz followed them there. A doctor checked the teens and said they were fine. Grace, though, needed to rest her voice for about a month. The doctor saw Grace's scars on her arms, and she told him that they were also from the burglar.

A week later, Grace found out that home invasions weren't common in their neighborhood. It was the first one in twenty years. Mr. and Mrs. Knotz put extra locks on the door. But, Grace has had nightmares about the man, dreams about the man holding an axe, chasing her around the house trying to kill her. There were nights where she couldn't sleep. Horror movies were still banned in the house. Grace knew this. She knew that if someone broke in again… she would kill them right away.

Later in the day, Their parents were out, running errands. Grace Knotz went into the guest room and looked through the movie stack. She grabbed *Psycho Killer* and opened it.

"Hey, are you watching a horror movie?" Justin asked. Grace jumped and saw him at the doorway. She didn't hear him coming. Justin walked into the room. "Let's watch another movie."

"No, we're watching this one. If you don't want to watch, then get out." Grace said, folding her arms. She was waiting for him to put his hands on her.

"Fine, we can watch it." Justin sat on the floor, kinda hung his head, and said, "Whatever you say, sis. Play it."

"Oh." Grace sat down on the floor next to Justin. She grabbed the remote and turned on the movie. Justin stared in her direction. Grace caught his glance and saw him looking at one of the exposed bandages on her arm.

"I didn't mean to hurt you," Justin said softly.

"Really? Not good enough, Justin. You hurt me."

Justin stared at Grace with a blank expression. His lips started quivering and tears began to stream down his face.

"Wow, you're just gonna cry. You're really full of it, aren't ya?"

Justin still sat there, crying.

"Fuck you," Grace said, getting up. She walked toward the door.

"W-wait…please, hear me out. Please." Grace stopped dead in her tracks and looked back at him. "Okay, go on."

"I dunno why I do the shit I do. It's just complicated for me. Do you think you're the only one suffering? I...I just... I just need help." Justin broke down and sobbed again. Grace walked over to Justin and put his arms around his shoulder. Then, she ran her fingers through his brown hair.

"I've changed, Grace. I don't want to lose you. I don't want to hurt you like that man did. I-I'm just so scared," Justin continued, "What if that man comes back?"

"Don't worry about that. I'm gonna get you help," Grace responded, "We'll be okay soon."

NEW TEACHER

If this girl asks me this question one more time, I'm gonna scream.

"Is this like too much makeup?" my friend Janet Robin asked, "Do my shoes match my pants? Do they? You have to tell me!"

Janet wore a gray pantsuit with black heels. Her outfits always looked gorgeous. Unfortunately, it was me that needed to be gorgeous. My outfit game required serious work. I wore a chartreuse shirt with black pants and white sneakers, a size too small. My feet hurt with each step.

"They match," I said.

"I don't know, Alex. I may need a second opinion."

"You're gorgeous, for God's sake. Besides, be excited that we're going back to Ms. Langston's class."

"Oh yeah," Janet said as she started adjusting her puffy blond hair. "Like what experiments are we doing in her class this year?"

"I dunno."

Ms. Langston was our favorite teacher. She was hilarious; she told funny stories about her cat's weird antics. We also did the most incredible experiments, like homemade rockets, pasta rockets, and rainbow in a glass. She was the best. I knew that she must've had big plans.

"I just hope I don't get teased this year." As the official chubby girl, the kids gave me hell last year. Hopefully, there will be someone else they'll call Chubster or Chub Chubs. Janet and I didn't become friends until the last two months of school last year. She must've only wanted to be friends with me because I had no friends, plus she looks even better standing next to me. I think that she doesn't truly like me. But I was desperate for a friend—someone to talk and vent to.

I pulled out a bag of Cheetos from my pocket and gobbled them up. Since I was ten, I always ate a bag of Cheetos in the morning. Cheetos were my favorite chip. They were like orange sunshine in my mouth—pure heaven.

"Why do you eat that junk in the morning?" Janet asked. She wasn't looking at me. But through her compact, she held up to her face. She was admiring her face through it, probably checking to see if she put on enough makeup. I saw my chubby self through her reflection. "Um, excuse me these are the best chips. I'm not waiting until lunch to eat them."

"Weird," Janet mouthed to herself, still looking at herself through the mirror as we walked. I finished the bag of Cheetos, crumpled up the bag, and tossed it on the street. As I walked, I admired Janet's beauty. Janet was built like a supermodel. She was tall and regal with the most perfect teacup boobs. Her thin body shape was curvy in the right spots. She had my dream body. Janet had blond curly hair and the most sparkly blue eyes that shined like diamonds. About half the guys at school wanted her. No boy wanted me.

Ms. Langston was the only teacher I liked. She said I was her favorite student. The only teacher that genuinely appreciated my big tub of lard ass. I was more excited than Janet to go back to her class. So many kids were walking in, and parents were flooding the parking lot as we approached Douglass High. As we walked up the steps to the main door, a red-haired boy shouted, "Hey, fatso! There are burgers in the parking lot!"

I ignored him and continued walking. I started to tear up. The bullying was just sickening. To make it even worse, Janet didn't even defend me. Which is why I thought she wasn't my friend.

"Why didn't you defend me against that guy?" I asked.

"Oh, aw, I didn't think he was talking to you," Janet said.

We got inside the school and headed up to the classroom. Ms. Langston wasn't there. Instead, a tall, skinny lady with brown hair was in the back of the classroom, organizing her desk. She beamed at me. She seemed to be in awe of me. The lady had a pointy hook nose and black-rimmed glasses. Her smile faded, and she growled, "Sit,"

I sat down at a desk. *What a greeting. But where was Ms. Langston? Is she sick? Did she leave? Is she replacing Ms. Langston? If she is, what if she hates me? Ms. Langston was the only teacher that ever truly liked me.* So many thoughts raced through my mind. "What happened to Ms. Langston?" I asked the lady.

She shrugged and said, "Beats me."

Janet and I stared at each other wide-eyed. Where was Ms. Langston? The bell rang, and kids flooded into the classroom. The lady came to the front of the classroom.

"I'm Ms. Anderson. You look like fine victims, oh I mean students," She chuckled. I sat there bewildered. Victims? What did she mean by that? Ms. Anderson stared at me. Then, she walked up to my desk and brought her face close to mine. I could smell her hot breath. "You're going to be my favvvvvorite student," she said softly. Ms. Anderson's eyes seemed to fill with hunger; they didn't blink. It was almost like they could eat me.

"Cool," I replied nervously. *How can you be my favorite student? I'm too fat. Why do you like me? The fuck?* Ms. Anderson started drooling. Eww, It drizzled out of her mouth on my desk. Her unblinking eyes locked on mine. She appeared to be in some sort of trance. What. The. Actual. Fuck.

"Ms. Anderson, you ok?" I asked. "You're drooling," She blinked several times.

"Oh," she said. Ms. Anderson stumbled back to the front of the classroom. She wiped the drool with the back of her hand. "Uh, w-well ok. I-I'm going to hand out textbooks now."

Ms. Anderson went to the back of the room and grabbed the stack of textbooks. She stopped and stared at the Xavier Brothers' desks. Jace and Amos Xavier weren't brothers, but we called them that because they had the same last name. Jace and Amos were chubby, like me, I think even heavier than I was. I saw them get their fair share of body shaming in the hallways as well.

Ms. Anderson's eyes grew wide at them. They didn't blink. She was under that trance again.

"Why, you two have such beautiful bodies!" Ms. Anderson gushed. She lightly slapped Amos' rosy cheeks. Amos stared google-eyed at her. His brown eyes looked surprised. Then, he turned and gave the same look to Jace. Jace shrugged his shoulders.

"Uh…thanks?" Amos said.

Ms. Anderson came closer and examined Jace. She gave him a tiny pinch on the arm.

"I can't wait to eat you–oh I mean–teach you!"

Amos and Jace's expressions changed, and they began to burst out laughing. "Good, one, new teacher," Jace said. Ms. Anderson's eyes went back to their normal size, and her smile turned into a scowl. She went back to the front of the room.

"Open up your textbooks to Chapter 13. I think that's where Ms. Langston left off last year, right?

* * *

Throughout the rest of class, we worked in our textbooks. It seemed like Ms. Anderson didn't even know what she was doing. She would stumble on her words a lot. She'd state incorrect facts; it was so embarrassing. One of the students had to give her the correct definition of a mitochondria. What was even creepier was that Ms. Anderson constantly gave me and the Xavier Brothers weird stares while she taught. Why was she so attracted to me? I was too big and fat, for God's sake. One couldn't describe the excitement I felt when the lunch bell rang.

"I think Ms. Anderson is like creepy," Janet said, twirling her fork in her chicken salad.

"She drooled on me like an afternoon snack." I didn't know what was wrong with her. The incident in class was so disturbing. She acted like she wanted to eat me. "I miss Ms. Langston already," I said.

"I like wonder where she went," Janet said, sipping her Coke. "Maybe Ms. Anderson is a substitute,"

That couldn't be. Ms. Anderson couldn't be a substitute. She said she didn't know where Ms. Langston went. Even worse, Ms. Anderson never said she was.

"Is this like... the right lipstick color for me?" Janet asked. She had on turquoise lipstick.

"Yes, it is. It compliments your hair."

"Don't be funny. This color is like horrible."

Oh lord, here she goes.

"Janet, it's amazing, for goodness sakes! Goddamn!" I swear to God, Janet was always doing this. It annoyed me.

Janet always looked good, and she knew it. I didn't understand why she was acting all insecure. It was me who needed to be insecure. I was a big tub of lard, for fuck sake.

"Like calm down. I'll keep it on, I guess." Janet said.

No, you won't. The lipstick will be off by the next period.

I opened up my lunchbox for the first time during lunch. Inside were two sandwiches, two fruit roll-ups, two strawberry yogurts, and a Nutter Butter. My mom always packed my lunch. She always gave me a lot of food. That was one of the only things I liked about her. I unwrapped one of the sandwiches and took a big bite. "I... think... Ms. Langston quit," I said as she chewed. But I wasn't so sure *that* was the answer.

"I don't think so. Ms. Langston seemed to love teaching. She said she would never quit." She was right. None of it added up.

"Oh crap, do you like to have a pencil? I have to do the history homework." She always bummed me for pencils. She still owed me three from last year! I looked through my things and saw my pencil case wasn't there.

"Oh no, I left my case in Ms. Anderson's room," I said.

"Like go get it."

I told the lunchroom monitor, Debbie, where I was going. She said yes, and I raced upstairs. I walked down the hall and got to her room. I could see Ms. Anderson through the glass window on the door. She was sitting at her desk, rummaging through her purse. She pulled out two jars full of live ants and giant cockroaches. Could those be for a project? Ms. Anderson opened a jar and grabbed a handful of ants. They crawled around her hand, and some fell to the floor. What she did next made my heart drop. Ms. Anderson dropped the ants into her gaping mouth and munched on them. I heard her smacking hungrily. I struggled to keep my lunch down. She swallowed them and licked more from her fingers. "Yummy! Yummy!" I heard her say through the window.

Ms. Anderson opened the jar of live cockroaches. But this time, she poured cockroaches from a jar into her mouth. She emptied the jar and chomped and chomped and chomped on them. "Yummy! Yummy! Yummy!" She chanted. Spittle flew from her mouth as she chewed. Her face lit up in satisfaction. Within a few seconds, Ms. Anderson had swallowed the cockroaches. Her grin grew wider. I dashed out of there quickly but didn't make it too far. Fuck, I was too chubby to even run for long periods. I speed walked downstairs and headed to Principal Warren's office. *Who is Ms. Anderson? Is she a… monster? What is she?* I thought. I got to the principal's office and went inside. Principal Warren was typing away on his computer. He flashed me a grin.

"Hi Alexandra, why aren't you at lunch," he asked.

"M-Mrs. Anderson's a monster! She ate ants and roaches!" Principal Warren narrowed his eyes at me through his glasses and asked, "The new science teacher?"

New science teacher?

Then she *is* replacing Ms. Langston. "Yes, she's a monster!" I yelled. He continued to stare at me with a look of disbelief on his face. He was struggling to believe me. His expression changed to anger.

"How dare you come in here and make up some wild tale!" Principal Warren bellowed.

"B-b-but it's true,"

"You have detention after school. Get out," he said coldly. I tried to speak, but no sound came out.

"Out of my office!" Principal Warren made shooing motions with his hand, the same way to shoo away a dog. I obeyed and walked out of the office. Why didn't he believe me? Worse, I couldn't believe that Ms. Langston quit her job. Why? After detention, I walked out of school. Principal Warren had called my parents. I knew I was in for it once I got home.

I walked out of the school and onto the sidewalk. No one else was around. There were barely any cars in the parking lot. As I walked, I saw Ms. Anderson at the end of the block, walking with the Xavier Brothers. At least, I thought it was them. I recognized their unkempt brown hair. *Where are they going? Where the hell is she taking him?* They disappeared down the block. I walked in the opposite direction. Weird.

Finally, I arrived at my home. I used my key and opened up the door. The whiff of cigarette smoke and the strong smell of whiskey wafted up to my nose. The smell came from the living room. I walked into the living room. Oh no. Dad laid on the couch with a glazed-over look in his brown eyes. They were half-closed. His clothes were wrinkled, and there were stains all over them. Uh-oh. Dad had been drinking too much that day. He stared at me and didn't say a word. It was quiet in the room except for the low sound of the TV playing.

"Why the hell the school call me?" Mom's cold voice said from behind me. I spun around, and Mom stood in the doorway of the kitchen. She was fat like me. Her whole body blocked the narrow kitchen doorway.

"I'm waiting for your answer. Why the hell the school call me?"

"Mom, I know this sounds crazy. We got a new science teacher today named Ms. Anderson. At lunch, I had to get my pencil case but when I went to her classroom, I saw her eat ants and roaches. She's some sort of monster, you just gotta believe me."

Mom stared at me. Her cold stare turned into a smirk. She slowly clapped her hands.

"Silly girl, making up stories," she said.

"I'm not making it up."

"No wonder your fatass doesn't have any friends."

"But Ma!"

"Shut up!"

Mom looked at me up and down.

"I don't know why you wear that tight ass shit all the time. You look like a fucking pig. That's why you ugly."

Tears began to stream down my face. "I-it's not tight." I sobbed.

"Don't you talk back to me, little girl. Don't you talk back to me." Mom said. She held up her fist. "Or else you'll end up in the emergency room."

I couldn't hold the tears in. They all came pouring out. I wailed like a baby.

"Take your fatass up to your room. Don't come out until I say so."

"Yes, mam!" I said through choked sobs. I dashed upstairs to my room, still crying.

"All that crying isn't gonna help shit!" Mom called after me. I got to my room and jumped in, and cried. She always did this. She always did this nasty shit to me. I didn't know why she did it. I just didn't know.

Quietly, I got out of my bed and kneeled and searched under it. I pulled out a box that was filled with candy. It was my secret candy stash. I kept all kinds of candy there. There were Snickers, Skittles, M&Ms, the whole gamut. I opened up a Snickers bar and chewed it.

The Snickers bar was like chocolate heaven. All of my sad thoughts just went away. Everything that happened downstairs went away. I wasn't thinking about it and not thinking about Ms. Anderson eating ants and roaches or all the teasing that happened at school today. My tears settled. That was the magic of food. I knew that I wasn't supposed to be eating this. Food got me through some shit. Food was my everything. I grabbed a pack of Skittles out of the box and gobbled all of them in my mouth. I chewed and chewed and swallowed. I knew that the food was terrible for me. But I couldn't contain myself. Food was my actual best friend.

* * *

At dinner time, we had T-bone steaks with mashed potatoes. My favorite. Not tonight. The frightening image of Mrs. Anderson eating those bugs came back to me. I felt like puking my organs out onto the dinner table. But I didn't.

Dad still was passed out on the couch. It was just Mom and I at the dinner table. He must've drunk at least one and a half bottles of that whiskey. He was on vacation from work but to me also from life. All he did was go drinking and go to parties. He had to go back to work tomorrow.

"Alexandra, why aren't you eating?" Mom asked, "I didn't spend time cooking it for you not to eat it."

"I'm not hungry."

"Alexandra Stinson, you eat right now!"

"But I'm not hungry!"

"Eat! Eat! I didn't slave over a hot stove for you not to eat! So eat up, my little piggy!" Mom said, banging her fists against the table.

"I can't eat. Ms. Anderson ate ants and roaches. I saw her! It was so gross!" Mom fell silent and just stared at me for the longest time.

"You must've imagined it," Mom finally said.

"I didn't!"

"Who are you hollering at?"

I gulped and uttered, "Nobody."

"That's what I thought." Mom picked up her T-bone steak and put it on my plate.

"You gotta eat that one too, now."

"Ok," I said, as tears were running down my face again.

"Clean this shit up when you done," Mom said. She left the kitchen, leaving me in tears. I started to cut a piece off of a steak, popped it in my mouth, and chewed. Even when I didn't want to eat, I ate. I couldn't control my cravings. The food was just so good.

Once I finished eating, I stomped up to my room. My mother wouldn't believe me. All she did was bully and hurt me. What kind of parents do that kind of shit?

* * *

"Why did you call me?" Janet asked over the phone. "I was like busy getting ready to go to the movies. I can't like decide whether I should wear a green shirt or a purple shirt. Give me your opinion."

"Forget the shirt, Janet. I need to talk to you. I saw something horrifying during lunch." I said.

"Oh ya, where were you during lunch? You never came back. Thanks to you, I couldn't hand in my history homework."

She has to be kidding me.

"Ms. Anderson is a monster. She was eating bugs!"

"Gross. But I don't like believe you."

"I'm serious, she was eating them,"

"You were probably like seeing things," Janet said.. "Your eyes were like playing tricks on you,"

"You don't believe me either," I groaned.

"I like gotta go anyway. Alexis and Dean are waiting for me, and I'm not dressed. I'm gonna look so ugly. All thanks to you."

"Fine."

Janet hung up. I sprawled on my bed and stared up at the ceiling. Neither Janet, Principal Warren, or my Mom believed me. But I know what I saw.

I didn't want to go to Mrs. Anderson's class tomorrow. I didn't want to go to school. Maybe I'll fake sick. No, my parents will never buy it. Ugh, I didn't know what to do.

Reluctantly, I came into Ms. Anderson's class the next day. She was sitting at her desk, looking through a science textbook. I couldn't look at her the same after what I saw. The rest of the class came in once the bell rang—everyone except Amos Xavier.

Wait a minute. Where is he? I wondered. He was always here. He had flawless attendance. That was something he bragged about. It was so unlike him to be late. The last time I saw him, he was with Ms. Anderson after school. *Oh no.* What a horrifying thought. Did Ms. Anderson do something to him?

"Take out the homework," Ms. Anderson instructed. We did just that. Ms. Anderson walked over to my desk. Her eyes grew wider, making me uncomfortable like I was one of the ants or roaches.

She leaned in closer until we were face to face.

"You can answer number one," She said quietly. Then, she committed the most disturbing act of my life. Ms. Anderson stuck out her glistening pink tongue and *licked* my face like a dog.

"Ewwwww!" Everybody in class thundered. I sat there paralyzed.

She's so disgusting. I thought. That was such disturbing and abnormal behavior; I couldn't...

"You taste so good, chubby! I can't wait to eat!" She whispered in my ear. What the fuck. Ms. Anderson walked back to the front of the room. *You taste so good, chubby. You taste so good, chubby.* Those words haunted my mind. Tears filled my eyes.

No, don't cry, Alex. You don't want to be weak. Don't you dare.

I managed to hold back the tears. I wiped my eyes with the back of my hand. Ms. Anderson didn't do any more creepy things after that. The class went on like normal. When class ended, I went to my locker.

Back toward Ms. Anderson's class, I saw Ms. Anderson with Jace Xavier. They were talking about something. Mrs. Anderson had her face all close to his. Their faces were nearly touching. It almost looked like they were kissing. I saw her put a veiny hand on Jace's leg and slowly slide it up to his shoulder.

What are they doing? That's so fucking creepy.

"Earth calling Alex!"

"Oh!"

Janet stood next to me. "What are you like looking at?"

I pointed toward Mrs. Anderson and Jace. "Over there. Do you see that?"

"Creepy? They're just like talking," Janet said.

"Ughhhhh, you don't understand!" I said, raising my arms.

"What's like wrong with you?"

"No one believes me about Ms. Anderson! Not even you! You're supposed to be my friend!" I began to cry again. What friend Janet was. She was useless.

"You could be like right, but how do I like know you aren't lying?" Janet said. She began to adjust her hair again. She opened her small handbag and pulled out lipstick.

"Should I wear purple or pink lipstick?" she asked.

"Ugh, purple!"

"Nah, I don't know. I need a second opinion."

"Just wear the goddamn lipstick!"

Janet narrowed her blue eyes at me. "What the hell is like wrong with you today?"

"I'm sorry, it's just that… everything's hard right now!"

"Yeah, it's all like so hard," Janet said, sarcastically. Janet pulled her compact out and applied pink lipstick instead of purple. Talking to Janet was like talking to a brick wall sometimes. I stared in the direction of Ms. Anderson's classroom. I saw her and Jace, still acting creepy. Ms. Anderson had moved her face back to normal. Then, she walked back to her classroom, and Jace walked off in a random direction.

That was when it all pieces together. Ms. Anderson's creepiness toward me, the walk with Amos, the uncomfortable eyes, the drool. All of it came together.

"I think Mrs. Anderson keeps doing those creepy things to me because I'm chubby," I said. Janet looked up from her compact. "Like for real?"

I nodded and said, "Think about it. I'm the only chubby one in that class. Everyone else is skinny. You never saw her trying to humiliate them in class. She even said that I was going to be her favorite student," I explained.

"I guess you're like right on that."

"So what I'm going to do is to not go to school for a month…"

"I do like the sound of that."

"To get away from Mrs. Anderson for as long as I can," I said, "She's gonna eat me eventually. What I'm gonna do to make sure that doesn't happen is not to eat. I'm also going to exercise. I'm gonna not eat. This is a perfect plan!" I said finally.

"What, no, you're not doing that!" Janet screamed.

"It's just what I'll have to do. To get Ms. Anderson off my back. I'll be extremely skinny so I can be just as gorgeous as you, Janet."

"No, you're not doing that!" Janet screamed, "You'll get sick and you'll like...like... die!" The bell rang.

"Shut up, Janet. This is what I'm gonna do. You can't stop me," I said. "Besides, why do you give a damn about me now?" Finally, the bell rang. I walked away and knocked my straight brown hair back as I walked to Geometry class.

"Think about what you're doing!" Janet called out after me.

* * *

After school, I walked home alone. I finally reached my house and entered. Mom and Dad said they would be home really late due to a late-night business party. They had left some McDonalds for me to eat for the night.

I loved McDonald's. Unfortunately, I couldn't eat that fatty food or any food for that matter. I left the kitchen with the McDonalds bag. I walked outside to the side of the house where the dumpster was. As much as it hurt me to do it, I opened up the dumpster and tossed the bag inside.

Then, I turned and went back into the house. I went downstairs to the basement. There was a tiny closet in the back of the basement where Mom kept yoga mats. She used to teach yoga classes. I opened up the closet and took out the dusty yoga mats. Well, she hadn't used them since she quit teaching. I laid them out on the hardwood floor.

Maybe, I'll do some sit-ups first. I thought. First, I turned on some music. I put on a random Taylor Swift song and got down on my back. I put my hands behind my head and began doing sit-ups. I kept doing them, *You can do it, Alex. Keep going. Keep going. No mercy. No fucking mercy.* I got to like the fiftieth sit-up before I started to feel tired. *No. Don't stop. Keep going.* My body was tired, but my mind kept saying, "Keep going." I slowed my pace and got to sixty sit-ups. After that, I was going to do seventy. I managed to get through the last few push-ups with my limited strength until I finally hit the seventeenth one. That was enough for me. I went upstairs to the bathroom and stood on the scale. I was already 216 pounds.

The scale calculated my weight and gave me my number. I was still 216 pounds. Ugh, I hate working out. Why can't our bodies just let us lose weight after one workout? I didn't lose any pounds from working out, but yet I gained seventy just by fucking breathing.

I'm just not going to exercise. Not eating will drop those numbers for sure. I've heard stories of models losing tons of weight from not eating. I thought. I walked out of the bathroom, went up to my room, and laid down on my bed.

* * *

The following day, I had a plan for skipping school today. It was 7:30 a.m. I was just going to make up some bullshit story about wanting to go to school early. I didn't need to be there until 8:30. Then, I would leave the house and wait out in front of the big bushes in front of my house. Mom and Dad were going to come outside at 8:00 and leave for work. They would leave, and I would just walk back into the house and stay there. My plan was as simple as that.

I did my usual getting ready routine by getting dressed, brushing my teeth, and combing my hair. Then, I went downstairs to the kitchen to find Mom and Dad drinking coffee at the table. Dad was looking better than he had been for the past two days.

"Why are you up so early?" Mom asked.

"I have a student council meeting to go to," I said.

"This early?" Dad asked.

"Yes, now I gotta go."

"Alexandra, why do you have that tight ass pink shirt on?" Mom asked. She pointed to the pink shirt that said Love on it.

"I just wanted to wear this shirt," I said.

"Looks hideous, doesn't it?" *Yeah, my shirt said Love on it. Love that you guys aren't giving me.*

"Don't you want some breakfast, fatass?" Mom asked. "There's some cereal and Poptarts."

"No, thank you, the meeting is too important. Besides, they'll have food there." Quickly, I walked out the front door before they could ask more questions. I threw myself behind the bushes. They were up against the fence separating my house from the one to our left. I sat facing the driveway behind the bushes, waiting for them to leave.

Finally, 8:00 a.m. came, and on the dot, Mom and Dad went out of the house in their work clothes. They got into their cars and pulled out the driveway. I stayed low, trying not to be seen. Mom and Dad's cars finally drove onto the street and drove down the road. I made sure they were at least down the street before going into the house.

Then, I finally moved from behind the bushes and used my key to get into the house. My plan was a success. I was hoping that I wouldn't get caught. Later, it was around dinner time. Mom had called and told me there were fish sticks in the freezer for dinner. I went downstairs and grabbed the box of fish sticks. Shit, I loved fish sticks.

Should I eat them or not? I thought. But the picture of the fish sticks on the box looked so delicious. They were nice and golden brown. My mouth began to water. *No, Alex, no. no. You can't eat fish sticks. You're trying not to eat, remember?*

As much as I wanted to eat them, I opened up the package and took a handful of frozen fish sticks out. I needed to dispose of the evidence to show Mom that I "ate" some fish sticks. I went out the back door and toward the dumpster. I opened the dumpster and tossed the fish sticks.

No breakfast, lunch, or dinner. I got through Day Two. When bedtime came, I decided to check the scale to see if I lost weight. I got on the scale and waited. Then, the scale buzzed. I gasped at what I saw. I was 212 pounds. A four pound weight loss. It was good progress.

"Yes!" I said aloud, pumping my fists in the air.

The following day, I did the same routine of pretending to leave early and then hiding in the bushes. I avoided the leftover breakfast food and went downstairs to the basement to exercise. I decided to do push-ups this time. I put my music on and did the push-ups. I did about ten of them and finished.

* * *

Around noon, I was playing Candy Crush on my phone when I heard the front door open.

"ALEXANDRA STINSON, GET YOUR ASS DOWN HERE RIGHT NOW, YOUNG LADY!" Dad's voice boomed from downstairs. Uh-oh. I was caught.

The damn school must've called them and told them that I didn't show up for one and a half days. Slowly, I strolled downstairs. I came into the front hall where Mom and Dad stood, angry. Mom's hands were on her hips, and Dad had his arms crossed. "Why the fuck didn't you go to school today, Alexandra?" Dad asked softly. "The school also said that you didn't go yesterday; why's that?"

"I told you, Mrs. Anderson's a monster. She's going to eat me! So I had to stay!"

"You're lying. Your friend Janet also called us, saying that you were planning on not eating!" Mom said. I saw Dad take off his belt. Uh-oh, I was about to get whipped.

"Huh, are you listening to me, goddamnit! WHY AREN'T YOU EATING!" Mom screamed at me.

I couldn't answer her.

"WHY AREN'T YOU EATING? TELL US ALEXANDRA!" Dad screamed.

"Since when did you guys ever give a damn about me. Why does it matter to you guys if I'm not eating."

"Shut your ass up. Go in the kitchen and eat some damn cereal. Once you're done, you wait in your room because I'm gonna beat your ass," Dad said. I walked into the kitchen and prepared a bowl of Fruit Loops. Mom and Dad watched me from the kitchen doorway. I brought the bowl over to the table and sat down. I just stared at the Fruit Loops. I couldn't eat them—too many carbs.

"Eat that damn food now!" Dad screamed. I ignored him and just continued staring at the cereal. *Don't do it. Don't crack now.*

"I'm about to beat this girl's ass," Dad said. He ran over to the kitchen table and whipped me hard with the belt. The blow knocked me off the table. I laid on the ground, and my face turned red. That was it for me.

"Eat that goddamn cereal!" I knew that if I didn't eat it, I was getting another round. But I didn't care anymore.

"EAT! EAT!"

You gave me hell, and now it's time to pay.

Slowly, I got up, grabbed the cereal bowl, and heaved it at him. All of the milk splashed on his work shirt.

"Oh, you're. gonna. get. it. Now." Dad said through gritted teeth. He held up the belt and started towards me. I began to run out of that kitchen. But Mom blocked my escape.

"Where you going, little fatass?"

Dad charged behind me and whipped me in the back.

"OWWW!"

"Give her some more," Mom demanded.

"No," I said. I pushed her with all my strength from out of the doorway. She stumbled, lost her balance, and fell. I started toward the front door. I ran up to the front door and unlocked it. Dad made a grab for me but missed because he tripped over Mom on the floor. I opened the door and dashed out of that house. In seconds, I was running down the sidewalk.

"ALEXANDRA, YOU GET BACK HERE BEFORE I KNOCK YOU INTO SUBSPACE!" Dad yelled from the front porch.

I was running fairly quickly for being chubby. I wasn't out of breath like I usually was. In gym class, I can't even run three feet without getting tired. This was unusual, maybe because I was running for my *life*.

Finally, I approached my school. I stopped running and caught my breath. Then, I walked inside the school. It was all Janet's fault. Hadn't she not told my parents about my plan, I would've lost more weight.. Ms. Anderson was still going to be on my case now. She was going to eat me. Janet's so dumb. She can't stand to have someone be as close to pretty as her. This was my only chance to be as pretty as her. Janet was going to be the pretty one all the time, and I'm still going to be called Chubster.

I found that bitch at her locker. She was going to get it. I stomped up to her and slammed her locker shut. I looked at her and saw that...she was uglier than usual. Her blue eyes were red like she was crying; there were heavy bags under her eyes as if she hadn't slept. Her outfit choices were worse than usual. She had on a brown T-shirt with some pink yoga pants. Even I knew that was a fashion don't.

"Oh, Alex, you're alright! I thought you were dead!" She wrapped her arms out to hug me, but I moved back.

"Bitch, don't hug me. You ruined everything."

Janet stepped forward; her eyes were watering, she looked very hurt. I grabbed Janet by the hand and dragged her into the girls' bathroom at the end of the hall.

"What the hell, Janet. Why the fuck did you tell my parents about my plan? Why?"

"I was only trying to protect you," Janet replied.

I grabbed her right ear and held it, and said, "Protect me? I wanted to lose weight in a faster way. I wanted to be skinny and beautiful, so I could get off of Mrs. Anderson's stupid fat fetish fantasy!"

"Please let me go, Alex!" Janet shouted.

"You don't give a damn about me! Why the hell does everyone give a damn about me now! Whenever I want to do something, everyone just wants to fucking stop me! Whenever I'm not doing anything, everyone just gives me hell, and I don't understand that shit at all!" I shouted as tears came pouring down my face. "No one cares about me!" All of my anger and my sadness were erupting.

"You're beautiful, Alex. You're gorgeous," Janet said.

"No, I'm not," I sobbed. "My parents don't think so. I don't think so either." Janet wrapped her arms around me and hugged me. "I've been up all night, hoping that you were ok. I've been through the same thing that you went through."

"You had anorexia before," I asked. We unwrapped the hug.

Janet nodded. "Like, I never told you this. But a couple of years ago, I got an agent to be like a model. I was so happy; it was the best news I've ever received in my life. But my agent was...like judgemental is...I guess is like a nice way of putting it. She told me, I was too fat and that I'd never have a successful career as a model. She hated the way I dressed. She just didn't like me. That made me cry all night. I felt like I was not good enough to be the perfect model. So I decided to like not eat to make myself skinnier."

I listened carefully.

"But then, I felt like really sick, and I passed out. I was taken to the hospital and ended up staying there for like a month. The doctors had told me I had gotten like anorexia. I didn't want you to go through the same thing. It's unhealthy."

"Janet, I—" She hugged me. We both hugged for the longest time until we finally broke free. Like I said before, I sometimes felt that I didn't deserve Janet as a friend. Why would a beautiful girl be friends with an ugly cow like me? I knew why at that moment, because she really cared about me.

"I have like another plan that will expose Ms. Anderson," Janet said.

"What?"

"If she's a monster, let's follow her home and see what she eats. We'll get a picture to show to Principal Warren."

"What if we get caught?"

"We won't. We'll be sneaky about it." I paused for a second.

"Sounds like a plan," I finally agreed. "After school tomorrow, we'll follow her."

I couldn't wait to expose Ms. Anderson for the monster she was.

"Janet, one more thing," I asked.

"What's that?"

"Can I spend the night at your house? It's kind of a long story."

"Sure, thing Alex. I'll do anything for you."

* * *

The next day, school went by in slow motion. I didn't hear a word any teacher said. I kept staring at the clock, waiting to get out of there. Once the final bell rang, Janet and I rushed out of class, got our backpacks, and waited outside Ms. Anderson's door. The last group of kids flooded out of the classroom, but she didn't come out.

Come on, Ms. Anderson. I want to see you transform. Come on out. I thought. The hallway was clearing out—there were very few kids. Ms. Anderson finally came out of the classroom. She smiled at us and walked down the hall.

Her heels clicked on the hard floor. She got to the stairwell and walked downstairs. Janet and I stayed a few feet behind her. We got to the front door and walked out.

Ms. Anderson doesn't have a car. I realized. She must walk to school every day. We cut through a couple of neighborhoods and hid behind large hedges and bushes on the way. Ms. Anderson whistled and bobbed her head left and right. She turned around. Swiftly, Janet and I hid in a large hedge next to us.

Ms. Anderson kept walking. We continued to follow her. Then, we reached another neighborhood. We watched her go inside a tall red-brick two-story house. We hid behind a large bush. Ms. Anderson put her key in the lock, opened the door, and disappeared inside.

"Like what do we do now?" Janet asked. I ignored her because a light came on through the front window.

"Come on," I urged. I pulled Janet toward the window. We got on our knees and peered inside. I saw a refrigerator, microwave, and oven through the window. This had to be the kitchen. Janet had her head up too high. "Get lower," I whispered, pushing her down. Ms. Anderson came into the kitchen and opened the fridge. She pulled out a large aluminum tray that was about six inches long.

What I saw inside of it, made me almost puke my guts out. Through the window, I saw wiggly purple *worms* in the tray. They filled the tray up to the top. Ms. Anderson grabbed a fork and twirled the worms around it, like spaghetti.

She brought the fork up to her mouth and SLURPED the worms off.

"Yuck," Janet whispered. Ms. Anderson began to transform. Her eyes bulged out of their sockets; her straight hair fell out, her face became a disgusting green color. Her arms turned a sickly green too. Ms. Anderson flashed a creepy smile revealing a row of razor-sharp teeth.

"Oh my god," Janet and I both whispered at the same time. Ms. Anderson continued to twirl worms around her fork. She slurped them into her gaping mouth.

"Delicious! Just delicious! Yummy worms!" Ms. Anderson said with a gruff voice. She threw the fork across the kitchen, grabbed handfuls of worms, and dropped them into her mouth. Some worms dangled out of her mouth as she chewed. Chewed-up pieces of worms flew out of her mouth. I was so grossed out, I nearly forgot about the picture we needed to take.

"Janet, snap the photo!" I said in a loud whisper. Janet brought the camera up to her face and snapped the photo. Then, a flash of white light. Ms. Anderson looked up at the window. She glared at us. *The flash! She saw the flash!* I realized. Ms. Anderson walked over to the window and pulled us inside. Her grip was so firm, I couldn't break free. The house had a funky, musty odor.

"More food! More food!" Ms. Anderson said, "I got my appetizer." She looked at Janet. "But I can't wait for my entree!" She stared at me as drool came out of her mouth. "W-w-what are you going to do to us?" I stammered. She ignored me and grabbed our hands with an iron grip. She threw us inside the house. We fell to the floor with a hard THUD.

Janet and I started to go back out the window. But Ms. Anderson grabbed us and led us out of the kitchen. We walked through the living room and went upstairs. I struggled out of Ms. Anderson's grip but she was too strong. I couldn't break free. She dragged us to a room at the end of the hall. Ms. Anderson opened the door and shoved us inside. The room smelled so...rotten.

We screamed at who we saw inside. It was Ms. Langston. She stood in the back of the bare room, frozen and smiling with her hands on her hips. Next to her sat piles of bones. I saw some skin still on the bones on top of a pool of blood. That's when I saw the two baseball hats. The two Knicks baseball caps. They were Amos and Jace Xavier's caps. Ms. Anderson ate them.

"Great work, Marge, you brought them." Mrs. Langston said.

"Ms. Langston! We need to get out of here! Mrs. Anderson's a--"

"Monster," Mrs. Langston cut me off. She walked up closer to us. Ms. Anderson stood in front of the door, blocking our escape.

"You kids, you haven't caught on yet," Ms. Langston said coldly. "I'M A MONSTER!" She began to cackle loudly.

"A monster, how?"

"We both come from our planet Xarzas. Sent by our Commander to eat humans," Mrs. Anderson said.

"We wanted to go to a place with a lot of children. So we went to your school because there are many young bodies to feast upon. I threatened Ms. Langston to quit her job or else I'd eat her." She continued. Janet and I listened intently. Ms. Langston coughed and continued,

"So I gave in, knowing how she's much more powerful than me. So she locked me in this room. Ms. Anderson was just going to capture and eat all the kids for herself. She took my plans. I've been plotting for years. But SHE took them all away from me."

"Shut up, you dried up shit. I'm more powerful than you, and I can eat you now," Ms. Anderson said menacingly.

"Well, at least I was able to hide my true identity. These stupid kids found out your identity in two seconds," Ms. Langston shot back.

Wow. These monsters fight like some bratty teenagers.

"ENOUGH, I'm going to eat the kids now. Also, for those nasty comments you made, I'm eating you too."

"No, no, I promise, I'll behave. I'm sorry."

"Good." I looked at the door. Ms. Anderson was still blocking our escape. There was no way we could run out.

"Don't even think about it," Ms. Anderson said, catching my stare, "You kids found out our identities. You know too much."

"W-w-w-we won't tell anyone," Janet said, "We promise. We'll like take it to the grave."

"Please don't eat us!"

"Silence!" Ms. Langston and Ms. Anderson said at the same time. Ms. Anderson looked at Janet. "You're gonna be my APPETIZER! Because you're so skinny and curvy. You'll be quick to eat." Mrs. Anderson turned to me

"You about to be my main course! You have such a chubby body with that meaty skin, chubby legs, and plump face. My favvvorite! Ohhhhhh, I can't wait to feast upon you. I've been waiting a lonnnnnnnng time."

"Wait, I want to eat, Alex! Can I please just have something to myself please!" Mrs. Langston shouted.

"You can have Janet, and I'll take Alexandra. Deal or no deal. If you choose to be difficult, I'll eat you too," Mrs. Anderson said.

"Ugh, fine."

"Like, please don't eat us."

"It's too late. We're hungry. Tired of all this waiting," Mrs. Anderson and Mrs. Langston began to transform back into their hideous monster forms. They moved in on us, backing us against the walls.

"I can't wait to eat! I can't wait to eat!" Ms. Anderson chanted.

"No!" I shouted. I grabbed Janet by the hand and dragged her out of Ms. Anderson's reach. But we tripped over the Xavier Brothers' bodies. We face planted on the ground into the pool of blood.

Shit. I thought.

I got up and laid in a sitting position. We wiped the blood from our faces. Ms. Anderson started walking slowly towards us. For some reason, Ms. Langston stood at the doorway, staring at Ms. Anderson.

"No more of this foolishness. Just accept your fate," Ms. Anderson said as she opened her mouth, revealing all of her pointy and sharp-looking teeth. Ms. Anderson jumped so high she nearly touched the ceiling. She was about to land on us. We stared up at her in awe, knowing we were toast.

At that moment, Ms. Langston jumped in the air and pushed Ms. Anderson to the side while in midair. Ms. Anderson came falling, and she banged her head against the wall and then fell to the ground.

"Mrs. Langston, you--"

"I know. I know. You kids go downstairs and get a weapon. I'll handle her."

"No, I'm staying and fighting," I said.

"Do what I say! Go!"

Janet dragged me out of the room, and we went downstairs.

"Where the hell can we find a weapon?"

"Kitchen. In the kitchen!"

We found the kitchen. Janet started for the drawers. I looked on the counter to find something useful. Nothing.

"We can stab her. With these knives," Janet said, holding two kitchen knives.

"Perfect!"

"HURRY UP!" Ms. Langston shouted from upstairs. Janet and I dashed out of the kitchen and tore through the house to the stairs. We stomped up the stairs, three at a time. We burst inside the room to find Ms. Langston lying on the floor. Ms. Anderson was on top of her. Once, she saw us. Ms. Anderson began to charge toward us.

Janet and I held up our knives. Ms. Anderson stopped.

"Oh, Alexandra, you don't want to do that."

"Why not?" I asked.

Ms. Anderson let out a choked laugh. "Ah, you're so naive. You don't know this. Let's just face facts here; you're a weak girl. Always will be. You'll always be a fat girl. No one loves you. They all want you gone. I'm gonna fulfill my command."

"Alex, don't listen to her," Janet said.

"She's tricking you," Mrs. Langston said.

"Go ahead and cry. Like you always do. This is about to be your last day on Earth."

"Fuck you."

Mrs. Anderson's eyes bulged wide. I stabbed Ms. Anderson right in the stomach. Green blood began to ooze out of her stomach wound. She backed up in the center of the room. She held her arms up and opened her gaping mouth. Janet walked up to Ms. Anderson and stabbed her in the face.

Green blood began to spurt out of it. Ms. Anderson spun around slowly and did a whole 360.

"NOOOOOOOOOOO!" was Ms. Anderson's last scream before she exploded into a million pieces. Green blood splashed all over the room and hit the walls and on us. The blood stuck to our clothes and on our faces.

"Ewwww." I moaned.

Ms. Langston walked over to us and wrapped us in a big hug. "You guys did it; you defeated that pathetic excuse for a monster. I lied about all that stuff I said to get her on my side." We unwrapped the hug. Ms. Langston's green skin turned pale, her eyes went back into her socket, and her white-blond hair began to grow back. Finally, she was back into her human form.

"You were a hero, Ms. Langston. You saved us."

"Well, you two have always been my favorite students. But don't tell the rest of your classmates."

"We won't."

"Let's get you two home."

Ms. Langston walked us out of the room and out of the house.

"I'll see you guys later," Janet said. "I'll see you around, Alex." She ran down the block to her house. I made my first true friend since high school. I knew that I was going to be in for it, yet again once I got home. Mom and Dad probably didn't even care that I left.

"Not so fast, Alex. I wanna talk to you," Ms. Langston said.

"Sure."

"Well, first, I can't wait to go back to school and see my students again. You really helped me."

"Thank you, Ms. Langston."

Ms. Langston coughed and continued, "What was all that mess that Ms. Anderson was telling you, you know, before she died? That was hurtful."

"I-I just feel ostracized because of my weight, and I don't know why. Everyone, even my parents give me hell. I don't know why. I never did anything to them. I feel like food is my true best friend, though."

I paused, trying to hold back tears. "I felt like food is the only thing that loved me back."

"Alexandra! I think you're a smart and clever girl. Do you hear me? Don't let these fools tell you any different. You've got Janet. You also got me. I love you."

"Y-you do?" I stammered.

"Yes. Don't hate yourself because you can't meet these people's shortcomings. You're still Alexandra. Still beautiful and special, Alexandra."

My cheeks went pink, and I blushed. "Thank you." This is why I loved being around Ms. Langston. She was the only one who didn't see me as a revolting piece of shit. Instead, she had this little thing called Love.

"I'll see you in school then," I said.

"Goodbye, sweetie."

"Goodbye."

I turned around and walked home.

* * *

Of course, once I got home. My parents were furious at me. Then, they gave me my usual beatings. They didn't faze me anymore. I was stronger than them now. I know they didn't truly love me. But I had people that did love me. Not everyone loved me, but I realized that there were people that did. Those people were the ones I would be around more.

On Monday, Janet and I walked to school.

"That was like quite the scare," Janet said.

I nodded. "Yes, but at least, Ms. Anderson's gone."

"Yeah."

We continued walking.

"Ms. Langston's gonna be back teaching. Class is gonna be so cool again." I said.

"I know. I wonder what we're gonna do?"

"I don't know. All I know is that it's gonna be great."

We finally got to class, and I saw Ms. Langston at her desk where she belonged.

"Ms. Langston, hi!" Janet and I sprinted up to her desk and hugged her.

"Oh, hi, my sweeties!" Ms. Langston gushed as she hugged us tighter. We unwrapped the hug and sat in our seats. Kids came into the classroom; some gave Ms. Langston confused expressions, and some gave happy faces. The bell finally rang.

"Hello, class! Nice to see you all again!"

"Where were you? What happened to Ms. Anderson?" a girl from the back of the room asked.

"Oh, I had to take some time off. Ms. Anderson quit," Ms. Langston said. She winked at me. "But enough about me. Let's perform some fun experiments!"

* * *

Once school was over, I was sad. School was my only escape from home. I wanted to be with Ms. Langston a little longer.

"That frog experiment was so much fun!" Janet said as we walked home. I didn't say much. Once we finally got to my house, I stopped. I didn't want to go back in there right now.

"Janet, do you wanna go hang out?" I asked, trembling.

Janet saw my trembling and said, "Sure."

We walked past my house. I had to hang out with Janet just for a little while before I got back to my house.

THE WITCH'S SPELL

Sam Frazier pedaled his bike with all his strength. He sped through his neighborhood and rode toward town. *This fool better be there,* he thought. Sam was meeting his friend Jerry at *the* cottage inhabited by the witch, Clorice, who lived on the top of a hill outside of Newland. Kids in town thought she was mean. It was almost a rite of passage for kids to play practical jokes on her like, egging or TPing her house. It's rumored that if Clorice caught them… something terrible happened to them. Supposedly, a kid named Gerald was caught destroying her mailbox. Clorice cursed him. She made his head *explode.*

Gerald and his family moved away after that. Every child in town thinks they moved because of Gerald's missing head. Sam and Jerry were about to do something that would be better than all of the other pranks without getting caught. Without being noticed, Sam and Jerry were about to do something that was to surpass all the other teenage pranks, or at least that's what Sam thought as he pedaled through town..

Sam pedaled through town. He passed the barbershop where his barber waved at him through the window. Sam ignored him and pedaled past the coffee, ice cream, and toy shops. Eventually, he came to a large grassy area with a single trail to follow. Up ahead was the hill where Clorice's cottage stood. At the top stood Jerry. His heavy eyelids began to drop over his shiny hazel eyes as his curly mop top shook back and forth in amusement. He puffed a cigarette and let the smoke fly in the air. The air blew in Sam's direction which made him cough. He got off his bike and stomped up the hill.

"Did you bring the spray paint? "If you didn't, I'm beating your ass," Sam announced.

"I-i-i have it," Jerry stammered as he handed him a can of red spray paint.

Sam snatched it out of his hand. "Finally, the only thing you've done right all week."

"Can we just go? I know Clorice is a mean old lady, but she doesn't deserve this," Jerry said.

Sam sighed and forced a tight fake smile. Jerry knew he always did this when he got mad. "Fine, go then, pussy."

"I'm not a pussy!" Jerry exclaimed. His face turned hot red. "I just think that this is wrong. No one deserves to have their house spray-painted."

"Ok pussy, if you don't help me. I'll tell everyone at school that you're a Clorice lover. You know what'll happen then."

Jerry sighed and said, "Fine." Sam looked at the front window of the cottage. There was nothing but darkness through there.

"She home?"

"No, I saw her leave."

"You go in the back. I got the front."

"This isn't a good idea."

"JUST DO WHAT I SAY, PUSSY!"

"I-I'm sorry."

Jerry ran to the back of the cottage. Sam went to the front. The cottage was in desperate need of repair. It had chipping white paint and broken shutters. The spray paint was definitely going to jazz it up. Sam looked at the cottage, his baby blue eyes wide with excitement. Sam went to one of the front windows and sprayed a big red X on it. Then, he walked over to the side of the cottage and sprayed skulls. *Yes. Yes. This feels so good.* Sam thought.

It felt good for Sam to spray-paint the cottage. Clorice was a mean old hag. She often sat in the front of their school and insulted kids. Saying nasty things. Sam himself had gotten offended by her. She made fun of his clothes and the way he wore his dyed white hair as an undercut. Sam hated her insults. He often wished she was dead.

The thought of that made him want to kill her. Sam Frazier hated insults. He took his spray paint and sprayed the message in scrawly red letters, JUST GO KILL YOURSELF, YOU OLD BAG. Sam stepped back. The message was just beautiful to him.

"Check out what I wrote! Move your ass!" Sam declared. Jerry ran to the side of the cottage and looked at the message. "That's so mean," he commented. "Uncalled for."

"Since when did you become such a wimp? After almost getting arrested last year? Come on, get over it, dude," Sam said.

"Get over it? How the fuck can I just 'get over it' I could've gone to prison for a long, long time!" Jerry had almost gotten arrested last year when he was thirteen. He and Sam went to a tagged building and spray-painted a bunch of nasty artwork on it, including a message saying NEWLAND STINKS! A police car was coming toward them and Sam was already gone, leaving Jerry to take the blame.

Jerry didn't get arrested, but he had to do one hundred hours of community service. But he still hung out with Sam. He was nothing without Sam. He brought that excitement in his life, despite the crazy things he did. The boys continued spray painting. Sam moved to the back of the cottage. As they vandalized, they heard a bloodcurdling scream coming from the front of the cottage. The boys jumped nearly ten feet in the air.

"What the hell was that?" Sam asked, wide-eyed. Jerry shrugged. "Beats me," They dashed to the front of the cottage.

Clorice stood in the front. Her mouth was a large **O**. Her eyes bulged at the graffiti. Tears began to fall down her face. She walked to the back of the cottage for a minute and returned with a glare.

"You two will regret this," Clorice said as she stepped toward the boys. "Blisters all over you two."

"What the hell does that mean?" Sam asked.

"Now… get off my property. Get."

"Not until--"

"GET OUT!"

The boys sprinted down the hill and back on their bikes. They pedaled away from the house. Sam looked back and saw Clorice smiling at them in triumph.

* * *

Sam put his bike in the garage and went inside the house. When he entered, his mother stood with her hands on her hips in the front hallway.

"I told you not to leave this house. You missed lunch," Mrs. Frazier said.

"Fuck you, I go as I please. What the hell did you make for lunch?" Sam stormed past his mother and went into the kitchen. On the counter sat a glass bowl of Italian pasta salad. "Why'd you make Fisher's all-time favorite? He's dead! Why do we have to keep getting reminded of him?"

"Well, if you hadn't known. Today is his anniversary. He was shot on this day," Mrs. Frazier said as tears welled up in her eyes. She took a napkin off the table and dabbed the corners of her eyes.

"Well, you never make my favorite foods. So why the hell do you keep making his? We've been eating his favorite foods all week. Why?"

"Well, at least he was a good boy, damnit! He was smart, talented, and had a promising future. You were on a good path, too, before he died," Mrs. Frazier said.

"Shut up!" Sam shouted as he roughly grabbed the bowl of pasta, knocking it to the floor. Glass shattered into a million pieces. There was pasta with glass shards all over the floor.

Mrs. Frazier started to cry. "W-why can't you be more like Frazier?"

"I'm not Frazier. I'm Sam."

"Just get out of here."

"Gladly." Sam stomped out of the room.

"I wish it was you that died." He heard his mother murmur from the kitchen.

"Fuck you!" Sam screamed. He dashed upstairs and locked himself in his bedroom. *That bitch. Why does everything have to be about Fisher? We're just not the same. We're just not.* Sam sat down on his bed. a photo of Fisher sat on his nightstand along with Fisher's cologne. It reminded him of when he was six. Fisher sat down in the dining room and helped him with some math homework. That smell of cologne emanated off of Fisher as he sat close to Sam.

Fisher was ten years old at that time. Fisher was his everything; they played video games together, protected each other from bullies, and always got ice cream together. But more importantly, Frazier kept Sam in check. When Sam was twelve, his parents divorced. His dad took custody of Fisher, leaving him lonely. One day, while Fisher was at his dad's house. Someone shot him through his bedroom window, killing him. Sam instantly lost the ability to care.

Sam grabbed the picture, strided over to his window and opened it. He walked back over to his bedside table to grab a pack of cigarettes and a lighter. He sat on the trunk under his windowsill. He lit a cigarette and smoked it. Then, as if chasing Fisher's plethora, smoke flew out of the open window. Sam stared at the picture and cried.

"Why did you have to go and die on me?" he asked aloud. He thrashed and kicked his legs and howled, "UGAHHH!" He huffed and puffed, his face turned bright red. Quickly, he caught his breath and cooled down. That's when he noticed three blisters on his wrist.

Where'd those come from? I swear I didn't have them before. Weird. Sam thought.

* * *

Sam laid in bed that night, trying to get some sleep. He couldn't get Clorice's curse out of his mind. "Blisters all over you two," Sam whispered to himself. *What did she mean by that? Could it be a spell? Was she trying to scare us?* So many questions.

He tossed and turned under the covers. Right away, his legs felt itchy. Sam pulled back the covers to rub his legs. The itching seemed to burn and grow worse as he scratched. The itch grew stronger and stronger. Sam thought he would rip his skin off. He fought the urge to claw his legs that burned like they were on fire! Quickly, Sam turned on his bedside table lamp.

"Oh!" he shrieked. His legs were bright red. They were as red as a tomato. Sam started slapping them until he had an idea. He got out of bed and went to the bathroom.

He rummaged through the medicine cabinet and found Cortisone cream. The tube was half-full. Sam applied it to both of his legs and went back to his room. The cream seemed to ease the itching.

Why am I itching like this? Was it the soap? He didn't know why he was itching all of a sudden. He sat on the foot of the bed and ran his hand through his white hair. He always did this when he was frightened. Finally, he managed to drift off to sleep.

Sam woke up to the beams of sunlight shooting through the gaps in his closed curtains. As he was getting out of bed, he felt something bumpy on his legs. He stood then gasped. There were nasty pus-filled blisters on his legs. "No!" he screamed. How did this happen? How did blisters form overnight? Panicking, he ran into the bathroom. He touched a blister on his left kneecap. Pain radiated through his body.

"Ow," he yelped. Sam didn't want to touch them. He got ready in the bathroom and put on a T-shirt. Then, carefully, he put on his jeans— trying not to touch the blisters.

"Sammy, you almost ready?" Ms. Frazier yelled from downstairs. "Your breakfast is cold,"

"Coming ma!" Sam ran up to his mirror and carefully combed his hair. Of course, the hair had to be slicked back, or else he'd go crazy.

"SAM!"

"I'M COMING MOTHERFUCKER!"

* * *

"Dude, you look like death!" Sam commented as they walked to school. Jerry looked tired. He had bags under his eyes, and his hair was disheveled. Jerry let out a loud yawn.

"Well, you always look like crap. There is no difference today." Jerry rolled his eyes and scratched his arm. "I'm itchy," he replied. "I don't know why. It kept me up all night." He scratched the back of his neck. Sam's mouth dropped open. The same thing happened to him too!

"But that's not the scary part," Jerry said. He pulled up his pant leg, revealing pus-filled blisters all over! Sam's brown eyes widened in despair.

"It happened to me too," Sam said, "I was itching so bad," He showed Jerry his blisters.

"Wow," Jerry muttered.

"H-h-how did this happen?" Sam stammered. This was too scary. They continued to walk to school.

"Wait," Jerry said, stopping dead in his tracks, "I think I know who did this."

"Who?"

Jerry paused for a moment, very deep in thought. "Clorice," he finally said. Then silence. Those words slapped Sam in the face as he realized Jerry was right. He remembered Clorice's words and her smile.

"Blisters all over you two," Sam repeated her words. *That's why she smiled.* He thought.

"S-sam, your arms!" Jerry pointed.

Confused, Sam looked at his arms, and he screamed. There were blisters all over his arms. They were on the back of his hand up to his shoulders.

"They're s-s-spreading fast," Sam declared, "Oh my god, they're on your arms too!"

Jerry looked at his arms and shrieked. Indeed, there were blisters there.

"Ewww, I look like you. You always look bad."

"We gotta apologize to Clorice so she can undo the spell," Jerry said.

"And ditch school?"

"Forget about school, we need to go before this gets worse."

"Let's just wait. I'm sure they will simmer down by then," Sam wanted to believe.

"Are you crazy, dude? We must go now!"

Sam grabbed Jerry by the hand and said, "No, we're going to school. This shit could wait. I have to go to school to meet up with the boys." Jerry let go of his hand. "No! We're going to Clorice's house, goddamnit!"

"We're going to Clorice's house, goddamnit," Sam mocked in a babyish voice.

"SHUT THE FUCK UP! Ugh, you're so damn annoying. You know, it's all your fault; we're in this mess. You and your dumbass ideas! Why can't you be more like Fisher? At least he was cool and smart."

"I don't wanna talk about Fisher!" Sam shrieked. He began to walk back. "I'm going to school."

"You're just mad because he was better than you'll ever be!" Jerry yelled back at him. Sam turned around and stared at him, red-faced, and as quick as he began to clench his fists, he released them…pain and ooze. *These blisters hurt. Jerry has a point. Do I really want to live the rest of my life with these blisters? Do I really want to live with this pain forever? I brought this pain to myself. Now I have to fix it.*

"Let's go, Sam!" Jerry said.

Sam nodded. Immediately, they started running. They dashed out of the neighborhood and past the school. The boys reached the town, which seemed busier than usual. They walked past many people. A red-haired man looked at the boys, and he screamed. He pushed past them and ran away.

What's his problem? Sam thought.

More people walked past the boys. A family of three stared at them and ran away. A woman with black square glasses stared googly-eyed at them and dashed away.

"Why's everybody scared of us?" Sam asked while they ran.

"I don't know, we gotta go to Clorice's cottage fast!" Jerry said breathlessly. They continued to sprint. BAM! They knocked a lady to the ground hard.

"So sorry," Sam said. They helped the lady up to her feet.

"It's ok," she said with a smile. Then her smile turned into disgust. "What happened to your faces?"

"What?" Jerry asked, as he reached for his face. The woman rummaged through her purse and pulled out a makeup compact. She held it in front of them. Sam screamed at what he saw in the mirror.

There were blisters all over his face, forehead, cheeks, around his lips and nose. Of course, Jerry had blisters all over his face too.

"You two should see a doctor," the lady suggested.

"A doctor can't help us," Sam said. The boys ran past the lady and continued to Clorice's. They passed several other people and got to the end of the town. Finally, the boys reached the grassy area and saw the hill up ahead

"Come on!" Sam cried. They ran down the trail. Their feet slapped on the path. At last, they reached the hill. The boys plodded uphill. Beads of sweat flooded down Sam's face. His chest felt like it was about to explode from all their running.

Once they reached the top, they finally stopped to catch their breath.

"Made it," Sam said, through choked breaths. The boys stared up at the cottage. It was darker than usual and looked cold and uninviting. Sam and Jerry walked up to the front door anyways.

"CLORICE, OPEN UP! OPEN UP! OPEN!" the boys yelled.

Clorice answered it, smiling. It looked as if she knew the boys were going to return to her cottage. "I'm assuming you've seen and understood the pain of blisters." Clorice said, her voice as cold as the wind.

"Please undo the spell," Jerry begged.

"Pretty please. I beg you! Please!" Sam joined.

Clorice just stared at the boys, still smiling. Her arms were folded.

"I will undo the spell, under one condition," she said.

"What is that?" Sam asked.

"Clean my cottage."

"We'll do it." Sam said with no hesitation.

"Wonderful," Clorice said. Her smile faded. She opened up the door the rest of the way and invited them inside. It was dark inside the cottage. They were greeted with a foul smell. It smelled like shit. Clorice turned on a light, and the boys saw the mess. There were stacks of newspapers all over the room. There were empty TV dinner packages, jewelry, McDonald's bags, plastic bags, candy wrappers, and Corn Pops cereal scattered all over the hardwood floors,

The kitchen was no better. There were empty pizza boxes all over the counters, along with dirty dishes in the sink that looked like they hadn't been washed for months.

"This house stinks," Jerry whispered to Sam.

"Shut up, she'll hear you," Sam whispered back. The shitty smell was getting stronger. The boys realized it was coming from down the hall. Down the hall were two doors. One was at the front of the hall and the other at the very end. The boys walked into the room in the front and saw it was a bedroom. The bedroom was the cleanest part of the whole house. The king-size bed was neatly made, along with flawless white carpet without a stain on it.

The smell is coming from the bathroom. Sam realized. Slowly, the boys walked down the hall. They opened the door, and the shitty odor greeted them, causing them to turn away quickly. Sam turned back around and saw that the toilet was open and saw the shit unflushed. The sink was dirty and had weird black stains. The same odd stains were also all over the bathtub. Sam's heart dropped when he saw the spider crawl out of nowhere and crawl inside the bathtub.

"Oh!" Jerry cried.

"It's ok. It's just a spider."

"Spiders give me the creeps."

Sam and Jerry went off in separate directions and cleaned. Sam started with the kitchen, and Jerry began to pick up the trash on the living room floor. After an hour, Sam managed to clean the whole kitchen. He had done the dishes, and threw away the pizza boxes. Clorice wasn't outside when he went to throw them away. Sam figured she left for town.

He started for the bathroom. The spider was no longer in the tub, which pleased him. He got some cleaning products from the cabinet under the sink and cleaned the tub, sink, and floor.

Finally, the boys were finished about four hours later. They sat on the couch, tired.

"Hopefully, this is good for her," Sam said.

"Yeah, hopefully."

Suddenly, the dark black spider from the couch crawled in front of the boys, and it began to transform. It transformed into the gray-haired and slender-looking woman. Clorice!

"What the hell!" Jerry screamed.

"Nice job, with the clean-up. I was here the whole time, watching your behavior. I was testing to make sure you two really earned the blisters off of your bodies. Today, you both helped yourselves, not me." Clorice said, smiling.

"You definitely earned it, young fellas," she said. "Blistora Sectum Blistami!" A gust of wind brushed over Sam and Jerry. Then, they looked at their arms and hands. The blisters were gone! Sam touched his face. It was smooth as silk, no blisters! He pulled up his pant leg, blisters? Not a trace of them.

"Oh, thank you! Thank you!" Sam said, hugging Clorice. Jerry joined and hugged her. "Thank you so much!"

"You two definitely earned it. Make sure you keep those other pesky kids away from my property."

"Will do," Sam promised,. "Bye."

Sam and Jerry left the cottage. They turned back and saw Clorice wave at them through the window. The boys trudged down the hill. Sam was beaming. *I'm glad that I helped Clorice. I didn't realize that she actually lived like that. She was a struggling old lady. But I helped her and myself. I actually did a good deed. I need to do more good deeds. Then, people might actually like me again. I'll have as many friends As Fisher had. Fisher was an amazing person with lots of friends. That's who I aspire to be. All I did was insult others. Not anymore.*

"For some odd reason, I still want to go to school today," Jerry said.

"Totally. Let's get there fast. The second period just started."

The boys ran the rest of the way down the hill and off to school.

THE ABANDONED HOUSE

Ray Thorton was a scaredy-cat. His best friend Rodney King loved to scare him. Ray tried to be less fearful and be as brave as Rodney, but he always spooked him. The class had just ended for the day. Ray was about to pick up his backpack and leave. The students and their teacher had left the classroom; only Rodney and Ray remained inside. "Ray put your backpack down," Rodney said.

"Why?"

"Cause a snake crawled in it, that's why." Rodney stood there with his wide grin, revealing his two crooked front teeth. Ray thought it made him look stupid, along with his cleft chin that made him even less handsome. The only saving grace was his fluffy black hair. Rodney never told anyone how he kept his hair so flawless.

"Haha, very funny," Ray said, "Remind me to laugh later."

"Not kidding, serious."

Ray picked up his backpack and unzipped it. He shoved his hand inside. He thought he felt something slimy and scaly. Ray took some of his school books out of his backpack. When he looked inside, he screamed. His gray eyes grew wide, and the hairs on his pale arms shot straight up. There was a long green snake—curled inside his backpack. It stared at him menacingly, flicking its tongue. "Yaiiiiiiiiiiiiii!" Ray yelled. He dropped the backpack on the floor. The snake slithered over his schoolbooks and out the door.

Slowly, shaking his head, Rodney said, "Seriously, I told you not to look in it." Afterward, he laughed like a wild hyena.

Ray muttered, "You're rotten." He shoved his stuff back in his backpack and stormed out of the room.

Later, Ray walked home alone. *Why does Rodney think he's braver than me? Why does he always scare me? Why is the Mr. Perfect?* In frustration, he kicked a rock on the sidewalk. He walked past the Peters' House. The big house was surrounded by Fir trees and had broken windows and shutters. Everyone in town knew about the famous story about the murders in that home.

Five years back, The Peters' Family—a mom, dad, and three sons—were killed by two home intruders who tortured and killed the family. They say the family's ghosts linger inside, waiting to kill anyone who enters. This gave Ray an idea. He wanted to go into this house to prove his bravery to Rodney.

Ray felt better about the plan. Later, he called Rodney and suggested they go to the Peters' house and take pictures to prove that it's not haunted. Rodney agreed. They would do it tomorrow night, Friday.

* * *

Friday night came; Ray walked confidently behind Rodney in the windy night. The chilly brisk wind made his eyes water and blurred his vision.

"You walk too slow. Come on," Rodney said impatiently. He was six feet away. Ray caught up to him as they reached the front gate. The house looked as spooky as ever. Darkness surrounded the old house. There was a distinct aura about the place that gave Ray the chills. It seemed like the house was telling the boys to turn around and go home. Telling them that something terrible was going to happen if they entered. Shivers ran down his spine, causing Ray to have second thoughts. He imagined ghosts flying out of the windows coming to kill him.

Slowly, Ray backed away from the gate.

"You going in, or what?" Rodney demanded. "Do I have to drag you?" He sighed and stared at Ray with a look of impatience.

"Ok, ok, I'm going," Ray replied, "Just a little freaked." They opened the gate and walked up the front trail. The grass was long and uncut, but some of the flowers managed to survive the overgrowth of the weeds. The leaves crunched so loudly under their slow-moving feet any ghost within a mile radius had to know they were coming. Some of the leaves began blowing across the walkway, magically creating a clear path to the house. They walked up to the front porch and to the front door without saying one word. Ray turned the doorknob. Unlocked, another surprise.

"Here goes nothing," Ray uttered. The boys turned on their flashlights and entered the house. They came into a large entrance with a staircase in front of them. Ray shined his flashlight. As he walked into the living room, Rodney followed. There was a plush suede dusty rose couch, and an old TV with spiderwebs weaved around it mounted on the wall. Under the TV was a fireplace. Ray noticed something on the sofa. It looked like an old bloodstain.

"Check this out," Ray said, shining his flashlight over it. Rodney walked over and stared wide-eyed at the stain.

"Wow," Rodney murmured. They continued to look around. There was an assortment of framed pictures of Peter's family decorating the baby grand piano. In one, They all had big, hungry, wide grins on their faces and wore ugly brown sweaters. *So creepy.* Ray thought. He continued to explore. They walked through the foyer and shined their light into the dining room. The table was dusty, and the chairs were pushed in neatly.

The boys saw a doorway in the corner of the dining room. They entered it and went into the kitchen. Ray shined his light in the kitchen. It was connected to the living room. "Come on," he urged. Rodney followed. The kitchen was messy, the counters had weird stains, and piles of dusty and dirty dishes in the sink.

"Hungry? I wonder if there's something to eat in the fridge?" Rodney joked. Ray opened it. The stench of rotten whatever was in there hit his nostrils, causing Ray to turn his face away and slam the door shut. Like the house, it appeared the fridge hadn't been touched since the murders.Suddenly, they heard the front door CLAP shut.

Ray froze in place, only allowing his eyes to move, "Oh."

"Calm down, you big baby," Rodney said, "It's just the wind,"

"Well, it must've changed direction. Let's go." Ray remarked as he walked out of the kitchen. Rodney followed him, said, "Let's go explore the upstairs." and led the way.

Ray no longer felt the need to prove he was brave. He allowed Rodney to lead the way. He needed to toughen up and keep exploring. THUMP THUMP THUMP was the echoing sound the steps made as they climbed. Ray shined his flashlight in a hallway going two directions with many doors. They entered a room. Ray saw the artwork on the walls. The boys shined their light over the artwork. It was a painting of Van Gogh's *The Starry Night*. Ray saw another picture on the other wall. It was Edward Munch's *The Scream*.

"These are so cool," Rodney said as he admired the paintings. The rest of the room was unkempt. The beds were unmade, and the blankets were hanging off the bed. There were toys scattered along the floor as well.

"Seriously, this place isn't scary," Rodney scoffed. Ray ignored him and continued to look around. He studied one of the beds and noticed something poking out of the covers. He pulled what appeared to be a blood-tipped butcher knife.

"Rodney!" Ray cried, frowning, closing his eyes, and slowly shaking his head from side to side. Rodney came over and gasped when he saw the knife.

"It's so sad how this family died," he said. It was sad, especially for those kids who were five or six years old. As they were about to leave, Ray heard a muffled whisper coming from above.

Punnnnnissssh. Punnnnnish. Punnnnish.

"You hear that?" Ray asked.

"Hear what?"

"I hear voices from above." He pointed upwards. The whispers had stopped.

"Seriously, shut up Ray," Rodney declared. "You're just hearing things cause' you a scaredy-cat."

"I'm not scared," Ray gave him a playful shove to the ground. "I'm ready to go, now."

Rodney got up, "Just one more room," They both left the room. Ray said nothing. Rodney opened the door to another bedroom. Another room, which Ray assumed was a nanny's bedroom.

He shined his light around to find a plain unmade bed, bare walls, a desk, and a closet. Nothing interesting.

"We should just give up; there's nothing here," Rodney said.

"Oh now, you scared?" Ray challenged.

"No! Of course not…. It's just boring."

"Whoo, what a musty odor." Ray fanned his hand in front of his face then covered his nose with his T-shirt as he explored. Then he noticed that there were ripped holes and sweat stains on the bedsheets.

"Someone must've slept in here recently." But there was no answer from Rodney. The room was quiet.

"You hear me?" Ray asked; still, no answer. Suddenly, he knew what was going on, Rodney was trying to scare him, again. He tipped softly to the closet, chuckling to himself before he flung open the closet door. "Gotcha!" he shouted through his wide grin. No one in there. "Rodney?"

Ray looked under the bed. He shined his flashlight in all corners of the room. Rodney wasn't in the room. Ray was starting to get annoyed. "Rodney, this isn't funny!" he screamed. Where did Rodney go? Did he leave the house without him? Ray scrambled out of the room.

"Rodney!" "Rodney!" he called, cupping his hands around his mouth like a megaphone. He walked into another room, a bathroom. The dusty bathroom had a decaying stench. He walked out of the bathroom toward a door at the end of the hall. It was ajar. He pulled it open, only to find another staircase.

Another floor? Ray thought. Quietly, he tipped up the stairs but his breathing, like his fear, seemed to magnify louder and louder with each step. The stairs made a louder THUMP THUMP sound. Ray was overcome with frustration and fear. *Never should've come. Never should've come,* he thought. Rodney wasn't here, only dusty old boxes and trunks.

"Rodney, are you up here?" On the verge of tears, Ray cried out. "Rodney!" Then, he heard a whisper, dry as the crackling of dead leaves, "Ray, Ray, Ray," The voice whispered. It didn't sound like Rodney at all.

"Who's there," Ray shouted quickly.

A man's confident bass voice thundered. "HI RAY, I'M GLAD YOU CAME BECAUSE YOU WILL NEVER LEAVE."

Ray ran down the attic steps. He heard the voices calling from behind.

"Stay," a woman's voice whispered and sang.

"Stay," a man's voice accompanied hers like a duet. Ray ran down the hallway, dropping his flashlight. He didn't stop to pick it up. He stumbled down the stairs. Something grabbed his pant leg tightly around the calf, causing Ray to trip on one of the intermediate steps.

He rolled down the stairs head first.

"OW!" Ray wailed. Stunned, he tried to get up, but his ankle was twisted. As he gathered his thoughts, he saw a green snake on the step where he tripped. It slithered down the steps and stopped in front of Ray. Then, it slithered into the living room and disappeared. *That was close.* Ray thought.

He managed to pull himself toward the front door. The knob wouldn't budge. "Come on. Come on. Come on. Open. Open," Ray commanded. Then, five white shadows met Ray at the bottom of the stairs. They formed a tight circle around him, each with a satisfied grin on their face.

"What do you want?" Ray asked. He felt defeated as he dropped his head and paused teary-eyed before asking, "Where's Rodney?" What did you do to Rodney?" The family stared at him and nodded as if he should know the answer to that question.

"Seriously. Seriously, you stupid kids think you can invade our home," softly and dryly, the ghost mom said without moving her unsmiling lips. Ray held his breath, frozen in thought that this ghost was mocking Rodney.

"Just like the home intruders who did this to us five years ago," the ghost dad said, flashing a pretend smile.

"I'm so sorry that I disturbed you!" Ray cried. "Please let me go," The family's smiles turned into lipless glares.

"You invited yourselves. You invited yourselves to rummage through our belongings. So now we're going to answer all the questions you have about The Peter's house."

"NO!" Ray blubbered. They all nodded and began to move in…

"Stop."

The ghosts continued to move in. *Oh no. Oh no. I'm going to die now.* Ray thought. *What can I do? How can I stop them?* The ghosts moved in closer and closer. *Ghosts are already dead. I can't use any real weapons to kill them.*

"STOP!" Ray yelled. He got back up from the floor, slowly regaining strength. "You don't have to be evil! I was here just to prove my bravery to Rodney. We didn't know that the legend was true! We weren't going to steal anything!"

"Yes, you were. All of you kids are disrespectful. You don't care about anyone's privacy," The ghost dad said.

"But this isn't your house anymore. I'm not invading anyone's privacy because you're dead."

The ghosts said nothing.

"You guys are dead! Dead! Dead! No one lives here! Dead! Go back to the afterlife! You're dead! This isn't your house!" *I can't be scared now. They'll feed off my fear and use it against me.*

Ray continued to yell, "You're dead! Dead! You're all dead! Not in this world anymore! Dead! No one can see you but me! No one!"

"Stop. Stop. Stop," the ghost father said.

"Please stop," the ghost mother said.

"You're all dead! Do you hear me? Dead! Dead! No one lives here! You're gone! SO LEAVE!"

A gust of wind flew by, followed by silence for a couple of seconds. Then, the house began to shake. Ray fell to the floor. His vision was a blur. He could barely see anything. At that moment, Ray blacked out.

"Ray! Ray!"

"Huh?"

Ray shot up from his stupor and saw Rodney's face. He stared around. He was still in the dark Peters' house foyer. There was one thing missing. The ghosts. They were gone.

"They're gone! They're gone! I got rid of them!" Ray shouted as he shot up. Then he turned to Rodney, "Rodney! Rodney! Where were you? What happened?"

"The ghosts got to me. I wanted to leave the bedroom for a smoke, but the ghosts grabbed me and took me away. I don't remember where. It was just white. It was all just a haze, and then I just came back."

"Maybe since the ghosts left. You were freed from their prison," Ray said.

"We gotta get out of here," Rodney said.

"About that, You have to help me walk. I sprained my ankle."

"Sure thing."

Rodney brought Ray up to his feet.

"OW! My left ankle hurts."

Rodney wrapped his arm around Ray's shoulder, and they ambled to the front door. Rodney opened the front door with his free hand and walked out. They continued their small steps off the front porch onto the trail. Even though Ray didn't get the pictures of the ghosts. He obtained something better. Bravery. Ray Thorton was no longer a scaredy-cat.

THE VERY SCARY GAME

I clutched the board game in my hands. Couldn't wait to play it when I got home. I just bought *THE VERY SCARY GAME*. My name is Steve and games were my life. Video, Board, and Computer Games were my favorites. I treasured board games. Those were my all-time favorite because they were more old-school than video games. The best part about games was the winning. I could beat anybody in a game, no matter how old or young. I got to my house and ran upstairs to my room

"Ding dong," It will begin soon. I heard Mom open the door, and then my best friends, Finn and Drake came upstairs. Finn was a pale kid with two buck teeth and ginger-colored hair. The most tragic thing about him was that he wore an eyepatch. His father was a hunter, and he went hunting with him last year. Finn was careless and lost his right eye to the kickback of a shotgun while hunting with his dad. Since then, he's gotten used to using one eye.

Drake liked to dress like those 1950s greasers. Today, he wore a black leather jacket with a grape-stained plain white shirt. He had greasy slicked-back hair. Of course, he never listened when we told him he was out of style.

"Ya got a new game," Finn said, pointing to the box.

"Just bought it, and I'm so excited."

"Ok, bros, let's play before Steve has an orgasm," Drake said.

"Can I play?" a familiar high-pitched voice said from the doorway. I turned and saw Ivy, my annoying five-year-old little sister.

"Can I pretty please with a scoop of vanilla ice cream?"

"NO! Get out!" I yelled.

"Ugh, you're so mean!" She stormed out of the room.

"Anyways, let's start," Finn said.

Finn and Drake sat down on the floor while I opened the box. Inside was a folded game board, a white card, a dice bag, and three green cone-shaped game pieces. I unfolded the game board. It showed thirty squares in different colors. The first square was marked in big bold letters **START** and the last square marked **END**.

"This card has writing on it," Drake said, holding up the white card. We looked at it. It read:

This is THE VERY SCARY GAME
There must be at least two players
When the die is rolled, the numbers you roll add
up, and that's how many spaces are moved.
Try to survive…

Try to survive? I thought. *What did it mean by that?* I shrugged it off. I was going to beat Finn and Drake anyways. Every time I battled them in a game, I always won.

"This game is gonna be so easy," I said.

"You're going down, buddy. You're no match for the Drakester."

"Grow up already." I rolled my eyes. Drakester was a nickname we gave Drake when he was eight. He still called himself that and it really annoyed Finn and I.

We put our game pieces on the start square. I rolled the die first. Both of them landed in the center of the game board. I rolled a six and a four. Ten spaces. Suddenly, all of our game pieces slowly moved to the tenth square.

"Woah." We all said at the same time. No batteries.

"Why the hell did they do that?" Drake asked.

"I wonder why—" I paused and felt light-headed. The room started to spin. I opened my mouth, but no sound came out. The room spun faster and faster. I was floating. Floating. Floated inside the game board. I didn't see Finn and Drake. Everything went black. I smelled cedar. I was staring up at trees around me and even saw the sky. The sun was setting, the night was approaching. It felt like a long time before my eyes adjusted to the view.

Something bit me on the cheek. I slapped myself in the face, mosquito. It flew away quickly. Wait a minute... I'm outside! I had been laying on dirt. Finn and Drake sat a few feet away from me. They looked around with confused expressions. I brought myself up into a sitting position.

"How did we get here?" Finn asked, gazing around.

"It-think the game brought us." I saw the dice on the ground next to Drake and grabbed them.

"We're in the forest! The forest!" Drake exclaimed.

"Shut up, Drake," Finn said, giving him a slight shove.

"Heyo, bucko. You don't want none of this." Drake said in a fake New York accent.

"Both of you guys, stop," I yelled. I paced back and forth. *Is the game magic? How did it do this?*

"Look, there's new writing on the card," Finn said. We gathered in front of him. He was right. There were new instructions on it. I read:

You must survive the horrors you face or... You die.
To leave the forest, you must find the rock tower.
Once there, roll the die.

"Wait, we can die here," Finn declared. He started pacing back and forth frantically.

"Of course we are! It's called The Very Scary Game!" Drake said and laughed. Finn rolled his eyes.

"What is this 'rock tower' we have to find?" Finn asked as he scratched his ginger-colored hair.

"How am I supposed to know?" I gulped. What horrors were we about to face? It couldn't be anything too scary. Right? We were about to find out. Even if it was dangerous, I knew I was still going to win somehow.

At that moment, we heard a loud howl. It sounded like a wolf. The howl echoed throughout the forest, scaring away the fauna. Squirrels scampered, birds flew, and that's when I saw them in the distance. Five wolves with fixed glowing gray eyes trained on us. Ready to *attack*.

"The trees," Finn cried and ran. "Climb the trees!" Drake froze as Finn, and I started for the trees. We could see panic wash over Drake's body. "Come on, Drake!" I grabbed him by his sleeve and yanked. Finn stepped back and grabbed his other arm, and we rushed toward the trees. Swiftly, I started to climb up a tree. Its trunk was thick with many branches. Finn and Drake climbed behind me. I stared back. The wolves lumbered closer, about thirty feet away from us.

Carefully, Drake and I climbed onto a thick branch and sat.

"Help me," Finn said. He was frozen in place on a tree trunk. "I can't see the top." His eyepatch! I forgot he couldn't see correctly. I held out my trembling hand.

"Grab my hand," I demanded. Finn held out his hand and moved in a different direction s. He finally found my hand and grabbed it, and I pulled him upward with all my might. Yes! Yes! YES! He was climbing up perfectly. Abruptly, my hands began to tremble, and I felt my grip loosening. Finn began to fall back down. No! No! No!

"Help, pull him up!" I screamed at Drake.

"Calm down, killer." He said and held out his right hand, and Finn grabbed it with his free hand. I tightened my grip, and we both tugged him up with all of our strength. Yes! Brilliant! Excellent! It was working. We pulled him onto the branch. Carefully, Finn sat down. Closer now. The wolves were about *ten* feet away.

"We gotta stand up," Finn said.

"What. Are you crazy," I shrieked. "We'll fucking die!"

"Whatcha talking about, boy?" Drake said.

"I learned this from my dad. Just do it!" Nervously, I stood upon the branch and stared straight ahead, not trying to look down. Finn stood up and then Drake. At that moment, there was a loud CRACK on the branch.

"If we fall, I'm gonna kick you hard, Finn," Drake said.

Oh no! Please don't fall! I begged to myself. Finally, The wolves came under our tree. They stopped for the longest time. We stood frozen like statues on the branch. Finally, they lumbered back in the other direction. We waited until they were out of sight completely.

"Well, I'll be damned. This place ain't fo da weak." Drake said in a fake southern accent.

"No shit, asshole," I snapped. "I'm surprised that you even survived."

"You're the definition of the weak," Finn said, "That shit was scary."

"It was," Drake agreed.

"Psssh, no, it wasn't," I said. I actually was terrified. I didn't want them to know that. Someone had to be the leader of the group. That person was going to be me.

"Liar, you were the most scared of us all," Finn said.

"No, I was acting."

"Yeah, sure," Drake said. "You're…"

I didn't hear what he said. I turned around. Something in the distance caught my eye behind us. It was tall and gray and about ten feet away from us. The rock tower. It was as big as the trees!

"I think I see the tower," I said, pointing. Finn and Drake looked in my direction.

"What the fuck are we waiting for," Finn asked, "Let's go."

"Now!" Drake exclaimed.

We jumped off the tree and hurtled over to the rock tower. I pumped my fists up in the air as I ran. Yes! Yes! We found the rock tower.

We stopped directly in front of the rock tower. A yellow circle was sprayed around it, and the game board sat on a glass podium in the center.

"Wait a minute. Don't move. This could be a trick." Finn said.

"The fuck, you talking about, dude," Drake said.

"I mean, doesn't it look too convenient that the rock tower is just sitting here unguarded."

"Let's just go. You're overthinking it," I said.

"I don't know. I just have a feeling," Finn said.

I took one step inside the circle. At that moment, a laser shot out in front of me. I turned to the right and saw that the laser was coming from out of a tree. The laser had ended in front of another tree to the left.

"I told you guys," Finn said, "This was a trap. We need to go—" Suddenly, everything began to shake. Surprisingly, the rock tower, podium, or the game board seemed to move. Everything shook violently, blurring my vision.

EARTHQUAKE!" Drake yelled.

"You're making it worse," I screamed. Everything shook violently, I saw birds flying away and squirrels scampering past the rock tower. Trees began to fall. I watched them drop heavily to the ground.

"FINN, LOOK OUT!" Drake yelled. Finn and I turned around and saw a tree about to crush Finn.

"Move!" I yelled. I dove at Finn and pushed him out of the way. The tree fell with a hard thud in front of Drake.

"You alright," I asked Finn. He nodded and muttered, "Fine." I helped Finn to his feet. In the distance, more trees were falling. It was practically a bare forest. The only tall thing that stood was the rock tower. The shaking stopped. Everything was quiet. Silent.

"Well, golly gee, you were right, Finn!" Drake said. "I guess you a real smarty-pants, eh."

"Fuck both of you guys. Maybe try listening to me more," Finn snapped.

"Whatever," I said, rolling my eyes. We walked inside the circle and stopped in front of the game board.

"Where are the dice?" Drake asked.

"Oh, yeah. Here." I said, taking them out of my pocket. I handed them over, and Drake rolled them.

He rolled a six on both dice. The game pieces moved slowly to square twenty-two.

"Nothing can be scarier than tigers, right?" Finn asked.

"Of course there is," Drake said.

"Nothing scares me. You two are the wimps," I replied. Everything started to spin and go black. I opened my eyes, and everything came into focus. It reeked of seaweed, and I stared up at the night sky. I sat up and realized that we were on a boat. The boat glided slowly on the water. It was a small boat. Finn and Drake sat in front of me. All I saw was water.

No land. We were lost at sea. Drake held the dice and card in his hand.

"We're in the middle of the fucking ocean!" Finn shrieked. He gazed around in horror. "No. No. No. No. I want off this stupid boat." He stomped and stomped his feet.

"Geez, don't get your panties in a bunch," Drake said.

"Calm down, we'll figure this out," I just said that to calm him. I didn't know whether this was the scary part or the *actual* horror was about to come. I didn't want to find out at all.

"Look what the card says," Drake announced. Finn and I moved over to him and read the instructions:

You're still alive, eh
Not for long!
You must find the island to escape
TRY NOT TO DIE HAW HAW HAW

"Very funny, card man," Drake said.

"What's going to happen this time?" Finn asked. Drake and I shrugged. Finn shoved the card and dice into his pocket.

"How are we supposed to find an island?" I moaned, "We're in the middle of fucking nowhere." The boat started to glide faster. Water splashed on my face as it moved. I was beginning to get a headache from the strong seawater smell.

"Oh my god!" Finn cried.

"What?" Drake and I asked in unison. Finn pointed with a trembling finger at something in the water. His eyes bulged in panic.

"I-I saw someone smiling at me in the water," he stammered.

"Oh, lord, here he goes," Drake said, rolling his brown eyes.

Drake and I looked in the water. We gasped when we saw the faces in the water as the boat moved.

"What was that?" I asked.

"I-uh don't know," Drake said. After he said that, a figure jumped out of the water onto our boat. We screamed when we saw it. A zombie! It stood awkwardly. It had straight black hair that was covered in seaweed and wore tattered clothes. The face was grotesque and dirty like it had been in the water for decades or even centuries.

The zombie charged at and tackled Finn.

"Help me! Get it off!" he screamed. Drake and I rushed to his aid. We tried to pull on the zombie, but it was too strong. The zombie pressed his hand over Finn's face, trying to smother him.

"Get off of him," I demanded, pulling the zombie even harder. Then, another zombie jumped onto the boat and tackled Drake.

"Drake!" I yelled.

"S-steve help," Drake said in a choked whisper.

I tried punching the zombie in the back, but it didn't budge. I stopped. *What should I do? What should I do?* I thought. *They're too strong. They're gonna kill us.* That's when I remembered the game I played a couple years ago called *Zombie Attack.* In the game, one had to kick the zombies to kill them. It was a dumb idea, but it was worth a try.

I kicked a zombie, and it turned to dust.

"Woah," Finn said. I went over to the other zombie and gave it a hard kick in the stomach. Poof! It turned into dust.

Wow, they actually turned to dust! I knew my gaming skills would come in handy someday. And mom always said playing games was a big waste of time. I thought.

"Wow!" Drake exclaimed. But it wasn't over yet. A group of zombies jumped on our boat, giving it a hard shake.

"Oh!" We all cried at the same time. The boat tipped on its side for a split second and then straightened. There were ten zombies on board.

"Kick em' Kick em' It'll stop em!" I commanded. "This is just like Zombie Attack!" The zombies began to charge on us. We went in for the kicks. There was a cluster of zombies on the edge of the boat. I kicked them, and they turned to dust. Finn kicked two zombies at the same time.

"My knife! I'm gonna stab em," Drake declared. He stabbed a zombie in the chest. Blood poured out of the stab wound. The zombie let out choked gasps and fell on its bony knees. It touched the stab wound, trying to stop the blood from pouring. But it kept flowing. Then, the zombie dropped to the floor. Its mouth hung open, and its eyes were shut tightly. There was a large pool of blood on our boat left from it.

There was one zombie left onboard. It charged me—but before I could kick, it tackled me. It put its hands around my throat.

"Help!" I managed to yell. Finn and Drake came to my rescue, and they both kicked the zombie at the same time. It turned to dust, and that blew into my eyes, causing them to water.

"You ok, Steve?" Finn asked, helping me up. I stood up, rubbing my eyes until I regained my vision.

"I'm alright,"

"We were worried about you, pal. That zombie was really choking you." Drake said.

"I'm alright," I repeated.

"Guys, look. There's the island!" Finn said, pointing. Finn and I looked in his direction, and there it was. A single palm tree stood on the island.

"Now I think this shit is getting scary!" I exclaimed.

"You think? Were the tigers and the earthquake not enough for you?" Finn asked.

"We made it in one piece of a piece," Drake said.

The boat reached the island, and we got off. The game board sat under the palm tree. Finn took the dice from his pocket. We gathered around the game board.

"Hurry up and roll the dice!" Finn bawled on the brink of tears, "I wanna go now." I rolled. It was a five and a one. The game pieces moved six places to the twenty-eighth square.

"We're almost done. We got two spaces left." I said, pumping my fists up in the air.

"Woohoo!" Drake shouted.

We were almost done with this night-marish game. Everything went black. I opened my eyes, and everything came into clear focus. Red. I saw shades of red. A red ceiling, walls, and floor. The whole room was painted a bloody red.

I sat up and realized that it wasn't a room. Instead, it was a long hallway that stretched for miles. I couldn't see the end of the hall. The hallway was wide and spacious. Finn and Drake sat in front of me. Drake held the card and dice in his hand.

"What does the card say?" I asked. Drake looked at the card, and he read:

This is the last horror, or is it...

"That's it?" I asked. What did the card mean by "or is it..."

"This is too freaky. Can we hurry up so we can go home?" Finn complained.

"We'll get out of here," I said.

"Just chill the fuck out, Finn," Drake said.

"Chill out?" Finn asked. He had tears raining from his eye. "How the fuck can I chill out when we've been chased by tigers and tackled by zombies! How the fuck can I chill out? Why aren't you taking this seriously! All you've been doing is making jokes, and I'm sick of it!" Finn shoved Drake and knocked him down on the ground.

"Hey, stop it, guys," I said. Oh no. They were fighting. It was gonna be hard to get them to stop.

"I'm not a wimp like you," Drake muttered.

"WHATCHA SAY! I WANNA HEAR IT!" Finn hollered. He pulled Drake up to his feet and punched him in the face, making him fall to the ground. "YOU DON'T TAKE NOTHING SERIOUSLY!" Drake got up and ran to him. He punched him square in the face.

"STOP IT, YOU GUYS!" I yelled. Finn and Drake fell to the ground, and they started tackling each other. "Guys, guys! Quit it!" I tried to pry the boys off of each other. But they were too strong, and I couldn't budge.

"Shut up, Steve. You haven't been any real help either," Drake growled.

"Please just stop. We can get out of here. We just need to survive this last round. We're lucky to still be alive as is. So we need to just find a way out."

Finn and Drake stopped fighting and got up.

"We'll get out, I promise,"

"AIIIIIIIIIIIIIIIIIII!" Drake screamed. He began stomping his feet on the ground like a toddler whose mother wouldn't give him a toy.

"I JUST WANT TO GET OUT OF HERE!"

"DRAKE, CALM THE FUCK DOWN!" Finn yelled. He put his hands on his shoulders. "Calm down, man."

Drake started to calm down. He wiped tears from his eyes. Even though he was joking around before, I knew he was scared then.

"What's about to happen to us next?" Drake whimpered.

"I don't know," I said. Suddenly, a loud voice boomed throughout the hallway. It sounded like a PA from school. "Hey, you kids, the walls are about to close in, in two minutes!" a man's booming voice said over the PA. I looked around. I couldn't see where the voice was coming from.

"Now go!" the man yelled. Just then, the walls around us began to close in slowly.

"Run!" I screamed. Finn and Drake were already running. There was a square of white light (which I assumed was the exit) at the end of the hall. We ran for what felt like more than two minutes. The light kept getting further away from us the closer we got to it. I didn't know whether it was moving or if my eyes were just playing tricks on me.

"You got a minute and thirty seconds!" The voice boomed. I saw the walls were getting closer. They were coming fast. We had to hurry before we got crushed. To make matters worse, a group of about five skeletons jumped before us, blocking our path.

They tackled Finn and Drake to the floor. "Noooooo!" They pleaded. I rushed over to help them. I tried to push the skeletons off of them, but they wouldn't budge.

"Come on. Get off of them!" I cried. The skeleton's cradled around Finn and Drake like they were blocking them from me. I kicked a skeleton, and all of the bones fell on the floor. The other skeletons got off of Finn and Drake and started toward me. Their bones rattled as they walked. They had menacing expressions on their faces. They had to be mad because I killed one of their kind. Drake poked one of the skeletons with his knife, and it fell into pieces. Finn and I kicked the remaining skeletons.

"Let's go. Come on." I said. Finn and Drake stood there paralyzed. I grabbed them by the hand, and we ran toward the light.

"I see you defeated my skeletons. Let's see if you can get past my obstacle course of doom. HA HAHAHAHA." The man's voice yelled over the loudspeaker. A large hole opened up in the floor in front of our path. Inside, there was lava and four square platforms floating above it, spaced apart.

"We have to jump on them," I said. Swiftly, I jumped on the first square, and it wobbled under my feet.

"Woah," I tried to keep myself from shaking. I started sweating from the heat of the boiling lava. Finn and Drake jumped on the square, which made it wobble harder.

"YAIII!" we screamed.

Being cautious, I jumped on the next one. Drake did the same. Finn jumped, but he missed the square.

"Oh!" he cried. He held onto the second square with one hand. He was dangling on it above the lava.

"Help me!"

"Grab my hand," I said. I held out my hand. His hands kept moving off of the platform.

"Stop moving," I commanded.

"My fingers are sweaty! I'm about to fall!"

"Grab on!"

Finn held out his right hand and held on tightly. I pulled him up to his feet on the square.

"Whew," Finn said breathlessly.

"We gotta keep moving," Quickly, we jumped the rest of the squares without looking back and ignoring the wobbliness. When we finished the obstacle course, the hole began to close and disappear.

"You have ten seconds!" the man on the loudspeaker yelled. Immediately, we sprinted like we just robbed a bank. We were almost at the light. Drake tripped. He fell on the floor.

We helped him to his feet and continued to make a mad dash for the light. Our sneakers stomped on the hardwood floor.

"3"

We were ten steps away from the door.

"2"

Five steps. So close!

"1," the voice hollered. We jumped into the light as it closed up.

Everything went white. There was nothing but shades of white. The walls came into view. It was a room painted white. The door we came through had vanished. No voice, no nothing. I saw Finn and Drake run up to me.

Drake held the game board and dice in his hand.

"We have to roll now. I wanna go home!" He wailed. Tears began to welt in his eyes. We sat the game board on the floor. I rolled the dice, a one and a two.

The game piece slowly rolled two spaces. It reached the last square that read END. At that moment, there was a loud rumbling. Everything began to shake.

"Oh no, another earthquake!" I shouted. Everything continued to shake. Then, everything started to spin. Everything spun so fast, I only saw blurs of the white light in the room. I was so dizzy and nauseous. I felt the urge to vomit. As I was about to, everything turned to black.

Finally, I woke up. I began to see familiar images. Red walls, game posters, a computer, it was my room! We were back! I jumped in the air with joy. Finn and Drake sat up in the corner of the room.

"We're back home!" I shouted.

"Sweet!" Finn said, "Glad we're out of that nightmarish game."

"We did it, boys. We beat the game." Drake said.

We all gave each other a high-five, and we all began to laugh uncontrollably. As I laughed, I noticed the game board sitting on the floor in the middle of the room.

"I have to take that game back to the store," I said.

"No way!" Finn said. "We have to destroy it. No one must know how evil that game is. We can't let anyone else suffer through it."

"Finn's right," Drake said. "Do you have anything we can destroy it with?"

"Yeah, there are some tools in the garage," I said. We ran out of the room and downstairs to the living room. Our garage door was in the corner of the living room. We halted inside, and I began to look for Dad's toolbox. I found it and grabbed it off a dusty shelf. All of us ran back inside and back upstairs to my room.

Once we got inside, I gasped. The game board was gone. It wasn't on the floor where we left it.

"Where did it go?" Finn asked.

"I don't know," I said.

"Guys, look!" Drake said. He picked up a rainbow headband from the center of the room. It was Ivy's.

"D-did..."

"Yes, she did. She's in the game."

DOLLFACE

"Why do your sisters have that doll?" Vanessa's boyfriend, Jeremy, asked in the loud auditorium. He pointed to the end of the row of seats at her twin sisters, Amy and Jamie. Amy and Jamie sat there. Amy was messing with the doll's hair, and Jamie was chatting with a girl to her left.

"What are youth doing thith weekend?" Jamie lisped. She had a lisp problem since she was three. Her parents tried to teach her to speak properly, but she never retained it. The doll sat on Amy's lap like a small child. The doll was pretty with tanned skin, big rosy cheeks, and pink puckered lips.

"Birthday present. They're obsessed with it," Vanessa said and sighed.

"What's wrong?" Jeremy asked.

"It's just, I ruined the entire party. I tripped and smashed my face on the birthday cake. Amy and my parents laughed at me. It was a nightmare."

"At least the cake did wonders for your skin. Your skin is glowing right now."

"It's not a joke. I'm such a screw up."

"Don't say that, baby. Remember, nobody's perfect."

Vanessa sighed again, "Oh, I guess you're right."

"Ok, ok. Maybe we should go out on Saturday. We could catch a movie, whatever you want. My treat. I don't want my baby to be sad," Jeremy said. He gave her a kiss on the cheek.

"That'll be cool," Vanessa said. She smiled. Jeremy did make her feel a little better. At that moment, the school principal, Mr. Hawkins, came to the front of the stage.

"Good morning all, We're about to start the honors assembly. Most of you have done so well this semester, and I want to recognize those pupils today."

Everyone clapped and cheered. A teacher walked across the stage and handed Mr. Hawkins a stack of manila envelopes. "When I call your name, come up and receive your reward." Mr. Hawkins said. "Daniel Abbott, Michael Aden, Jocelyn Frye." The kids walked up to the stage to receive their certificates. "Amy and Jamie Greene, can you come up please,"

Amy and Jamie walked up on stage, but something weird happened.

"I don't want this stupid award," Amy growled. She took the manila envelope and ripped it into two. Jamie did the same thing and let the paper fall to the floor.

"Unacceptable!" Principal Hawkins screamed.

"THITH ITH UNACCEPTABLE," Jamie rasped. Both of them *kicked* Principal Hawkins in the stomach. "O-oh," he groaned as he fell to the floor. Everyone in the auditorium let out a loud gasp, including Vanessa. Teachers began running toward the stage crying, "Stop, stop out." But Amy and Jamie were punching Principal Hawkins in the face. They kept smacking him, causing him to bleed. A teacher pulled the girls off the stage.

"Girls, girls stop it right now," a teacher said. Slowly, Principal Hawkins got back up to the microphone.

"Assembly dismissed."

*   *   *

Amy and Jamie had to be sent home early. They must've gotten in serious trouble. Vanessa came home later that day and found them in their room.

"We got expelled," Amy said.

"Expelled? I bet Mom was pissed, wasn't she," Vanessa asked?

Jamie nodded and said, "We can't invite friendth or talk on the phone for four monthths. We even have to thtay in our room till dinner."

Vanessa really wanted to know about the violent behavior they pulled at the assembly. Why did Amy and Jamie kick Principal Hawkins? What possessed them to do that? It was so unlike their characters.

That was so strange. That was very unlike Amy and Jamie. Sure, Amy could be a tough case sometimes, but she wasn't a delinquent, Vanessa thought. She wanted to know what was going on. She needed to find out.

"Why'd you kick Principal Hawkins? That was horrible."

"Dollface made uth do it. She put uth under a thell," Jamie said, as she stroked her brown hair.

"You're seriously blaming a *doll?* I don't believe you."

"It's the truth," Amy added.

"Yeah right," Vanessa said, walking out toward her bed. She looked back at the twins and said: "I can't believe you would accuse a doll."

Dinner time was approaching, Vanessa was preparing dinner for her family to make up for the birthday party incident. She finished stirring the Shrimp Alfredo. It looked like perfection to Vanessa. She knew it was going to be good.

"Dinner time! Dinner time!" Vanessa shouted. Not even a second later, her family came downstairs. Her family, except Mrs. Greene, sat down at the kitchen table. Mrs. Greene dashed over to Vanessa and looked at her Shrimp Alfredo. Her smile turned into a frown.

"Oh my god, Vanessa, you forgot the red pepper."

"Oh." *Damn it. Messed up again.* "I-i-i'll add it."

"Don't even worry about it," Ms. Greene said, rolling her eyes. Vanessa sat down at the kitchen table. Amy set Dollface in an empty seat next to her.

"Amy, take that doll back upstairs," Mr. Greene demanded.

"B-but"

"Now!" Amy grabbed Dollface from the seat next to hers and got up from the kitchen table.

"Daddy is so mean," She muttered to Dollface. Amy took her upstairs then came back down a few seconds later.

"Really, I am disappointed in you two." Mr. Greene said. Mrs. Greene brought the food over to the table. As she walked over, Vanessa saw Amy stick her foot out and tripped her.

"Oh," Mrs. Greene cried. She dove forward, and the noodles and the breadsticks flew out of their bowls. The glass bowls shattered into a million pieces once they hit the floor. Mrs. Greene stood up and angrily threw a strand of her hair back and glared at Amy. "Did you trip me," she asked, narrowing her eyes at her.

"Yes," Amy replied. She and Jamie giggled.

"What's wrong with you girls today?" Mrs. Greene asked. They ignored her and decided to kick under the table, making it shake.

"Stop it right now!" Mr. Greene yelled. But Amy and Jamie got up from their seats and tipped the table over. It hit the linoleum floor hard, causing one of the legs to break.

"Amy and Jamie Greene," Mrs. Greene yelled.

The twins weren't done yet. They ran over to Vanessa and clamped their hands around her throat. "S-top," Vanessa managed to cry. The twins ignored her. They secured their hands tighter and tighter around her throat. Vanessa wheezed heavily. She knew that she didn't have long to live.

I'm going to die, Vanessa thought. Mr. and Mrs. Greene scrambled over to help her.

"Get off of her! Get off of her this instant," Mrs. Greene shrieked. She tried to pull the girls, but she was too weak.

"Die, Vanetha! Die!" Jamie chanted. Mr. Greene managed to finally pry the girls off of Vanessa with a hard pull.

"You ok, Vanessa." Mrs. Greene asked.

Vanessa clutched her throat and nodded.

"Now, what was that all about?" Mr. Greene asked, glaring at Amy and Jamie.

Amy and Jamie just stood there with confused expressions on their faces. They looked lost. "We don't know," Amy said, tightening her blue hair ribbon.

"What you did was unforgivable."

But Amy and Jamie just stood there dumbfounded. Tears began to form in the corners of their eyes.

"They need an appointment with a therapist ASAP," Mr. Greene said.

"I don't want to go to the therapith!" Jamie cried, "Dollface made uth do it."

"Up to your room," Mrs. Greene commanded, "We'll decide on a more severe punishment in the morning," Amy and Jamie obeyed her and sauntered out the room. Vanessa heard them sobbing softly. She didn't know what was going on with them, but it was getting too scary.

Their parents started to clean up the mess on the floor. Vanessa helped too.

"Get out of here, Vanessa. Leave your dad and I alone." Mrs. Greene said. She wiped tears from her eyes with her hand. Mr. Greene gave her a hug. Vanessa walked out the kitchen. She wanted to confront her sisters about their behavior. *What are they trying to prove? Why have they become so freaking horrid? What's going on in their mind?* she thought. It didn't make sense. Vanessa stormed into their bedroom. Amy and Jamie were on their beds—crying.

"Cut the tears," Vanessa uttered. "What's... *wrong*... with you...two?"

"I told you—Dollface cast a spell on us," Jamie said.

"A doll can't make you do horrible things."

"But she is!" Amy screamed. The twin just cried some more.

"Nice crying, It doesn't fool me or Mom and Dad," Vanessa said coldly.

* * *

At around three a.m., Vanessa laid under the covers that night. She tossed and turned, constantly trying to get comfortable. It was mainly out of fear Vanessa couldn't sleep. She felt uneasy about Amy and Jamie. Their violence scared her. *What if they try to kill me?* She didn't even want to be in the same room as Amy and Jamie. She wiped the sweat from her face with the back of her hand. *I'm never getting any sleep tonight.* Vanessa thought glumly. *I wish Jeremy was here. I just want to see his face. He'd tell me jokes until I laughed. He'd protect me from Amy and Jamie.*

She stared at the ceiling, hoping that it'll make her fall asleep. Suddenly, out of the corner of her eye, she saw Amy and Jamie getting out of their beds. Vanessa watched the girls turn on the light to their walk-in closet. She peered in closer to see what they were doing. Amy took something that Vanessa couldn't see. They turned the closet light off and tiptoed out of the room. Vanessa wanted to know what they were up to. Quietly, she got out of bed and followed them. Vanessa poked her head out the bedroom door. The yellow hallway night-light shined on Amy and Jamie's backs. They were standing in front of their parents' bedroom. Amy opened up the door a smidge and squeezed inside. Jamie followed.

What are they up to? Vanessa wondered. She tiptoed down the hall in front of the room. She poked her head inside. What she saw made her cry out. The bedside table lamp was on, and she saw Amy and Jamie on their parents' bed. Amy held a baseball bat up in batter's position, ready to hit her father.

"No!" Vanessa cried out.

She sprinted into the room and dove at Amy and Jamie. She knocked them off the bed, and the baseball bat hit the hardwood floor with a hard CLANK. This woke Mr. and Mrs. Greene. They sat up in bed, rubbing sleep from their eyes.

"What are you girls doing in here?" Mr. Greene asked, narrowing his eyes at them. "It's the middle of the night."

"Amy and Jamie were about to hit you with a bat," Vanessa said, pointing to the bat.

"Wait, what's going on," Amy asked?

"What am I doing here," Jamie asked, with a confused expression.

"Don't act dumb. You almost hit Dad." Vanessa said.

"Enough!" Mrs. Greene shouted. "You're all grounded for eight months, now get out of our room!"

"Me?!" Vanessa shrieked,

"You heard me. Now go."

Amy grabbed the baseball bat, and the girls went back to their bedroom. Everybody in the house went back to sleep. They were just too tired. The following day at around six a.m., Vanessa woke up to smashing noises in their bedroom. She sat straight up and gasped. At the window stood Amy and Jamie. They were destroying all of their Barbie dolls! Amy dropped a doll down on the floor and stomped on it with her foot. It was the Ken doll she got as a birthday gift. Jamie grabbed the Barbie dollhouse and smashed it on the floor. Vanessa jumped out of bed and said in a loud whisper, "Stop. Stop. You're gonna wake Mom and Dad" Amy and Jamie jumped in surprise.

"Why are you two destroying your dolls?" Vanessa asked.

"Dollface thaid that all the dollth were ugly and wanted uth to destroy them." Jamie replied.

"Stop lying to me. Give me the truth."

"But that *is* the truth!" Amy insisted.

"You guys have gone insane. What happened? How did you turn good into bad?" Vanessa asked, shaking her head. She tsk-tsked. Amy and Jamie burst into tears. Tears ran down their cheeks.

"We'll prove it to you that Dollface made us do it," Amy mewled. She ran over to her bed where Dollface sat, lifelessly.

"Dollface, come on, talk to Vanessa! Tell them everything you're doing to us." But the doll didn't speak. It just stared at Amy soullessly.

"Pathetic," Vanessa scoffed.

"Come on, talk! Come on, talk! Talk! Talk!" Jamie cried, shaking the doll furiously. Still no answer from the doll.

"I don't think I'm tired anymore," Vanessa said. "Hopefully, a therapist can fix you, nuts."

* * *

Vanessa walked home with Jeremy after school. "I don't know what has gotten into my sisters. They've gone absolutely bonkers! They almost tried to kill me!" Vanessa exclaimed.

"What they do?" Jeremy asked as he ran his fingers through his black hair.

"They choked me. They put their hands around my throat and tried to kill me."

"Goddamn. They need to get locked up."

"I wouldn't say that. They should get taken to a therapist."

"Well, if they try anything. I'm gonna end them." Jeremy said, clutching his fists.

That was what Vanessa adored about Jeremy. He was so tough and strong. In the ninth grade, He'd managed to beat up two bullies who were messing with some kid. He got suspended for it, though, but a complete victory for the kid.

Finally, they arrived at Vanessa's house and went inside.

"Mom, I'm home," Vanessa announced. There was no answer. That meant she wasn't home. Vanessa and Jeremy walked into the kitchen and saw a note on the fridge that read:

Took Amy and Jamie to the therapist.

"They've gone to the whacky shack, huh?" Jeremy asked. "Guess so,"

"Wanna work on that English assignment together. Mrs. Harris said if I fail this one, I'll be off the basketball team."

"Sure," Vanessa said. They went upstairs to her room. When Vanessa entered, she saw Dollface sitting on Amy's bed. She stared straight ahead with a lifeless blank grin.

"That doll is so fucking creepy," Jeremy commented. They both sat on Vanessa's bed as they pulled the homework out of the backpack. Vanessa and Jeremy started to read the article that was assigned with the English assignment.

As Vanessa read, she felt eyes watching her from behind. Eyes glued on to her. Slowly, she turned around and saw Dollface staring at her.

Weird. Wasn't she staring straight ahead when I came in? Vanessa thought. She was sure that Dollface *was* staring straight ahead.

"Jeremy, am I crazy, or was Dollface staring ahead," Vanessa said, pointing to her.

"She was," Jeremy said, "That's so freaky."

Vanessa felt a wave of uneasiness from the doll. On impulse, she turned the doll around.

"Don't touch me, girly girl," It cried out.

"AHHHHHHHHHHHHHHH," Vanessa and Jeremy both screamed. Vanessa dropped to the floor in shock but slowly got back up.

"Y-y-you talk?" Jeremy stammered.

"Of course I can, you fools," Dollface rasped. Vanessa rubbed her eyes, hoping this was a dream, but it wasn't—she was wide awake.

"Did you control Amy and Jamie and make them do all of those horrible things?"

"Of course I did. Your sisters are too goody goody to be bad."

"But why?" Jeremy asked.

"I love mayhem, I love chaos, I want everybody in this world to be CHAOTIC!" Dollface yelled. "The world is muucccch more exciting when there is chaos."

Vanessa couldn't believe what she was hearing. A talking doll yelling about mayhem.

"Why mayhem?"

"Enough questions. I must make you both chaotic!" Dollface declared. Her expression changed to anger. She started to mumble something that Vanessa couldn't hear. Then, Dollface's eyes turned red like a tomato. Her eyes locked on Vanessa and Jeremy.

"You wanna be bad, huh, Dolly! I'll show you bad!" Jeremy exclaimed. He walked up to Dollface, cracking his knuckles.

"I wouldn't try that," Dollface said. Her eyes glowed even brighter, causing her pupils and her sclera to disappear. Suddenly, Jeremy fell to the ground and laid there. He didn't say anything. His brown eyes were wide open but didn't blink. His body laid completely stiff, not moving a muscle.

"Oh my god! Jeremy!" Vanessa yelled. "What the fuck did you do?"

"You're next," Dollface replied.

No. No. No. I'm not letting her win! Vanessa thought. Without thinking, she threw herself on Dollface and tackled her down.

"Let go of me, or you'll die," Dollface gruffed. She squirmed and thrashed, trying to break out of Vanessa's firm grip.

"I will not let you kill me," Vanessa thundered. She tightened her grip on Dollface's shoulders. It didn't seem to phase her at all.

How can I kill this doll? What can I do? Vanessa thought. As Dollface struggled, she bit Vanessa's finger.

"Ow," She howled. Blood trickled from the bite out of her finger. Dollface managed to wiggle out of Vanessa's grasp.

"Hahaha, now I got you," She taunted. Dollface held out her hands to grab Vanessa, but she ran out of the room. Vanessa hopped over Jeremy and bolted downstairs.

"Get back here, girl!" Dollface yelled from upstairs. Vanessa tore through the living room and burst into the kitchen.

Abruptly, Dollface entered the kitchen along with Jeremy. Jeremy had a sly grin on his face, and his eyes were bright red.

"Jeremy, I thought that you...died," Vanessa whispered.

"Come on, Vanessa, be chaotic like your sisters," Jeremy said.

"Join us," Dollface said, "Join us."

"I won't!" Vanessa cried. She ran over to the side of the kitchen and scanned around, looking for a weapon.

"Join us, Join us," Jeremy and Dollface began to run to her.

"Come on, Jeremy, snap out of it! You're not evil! Dollface is using you!" Vanessa bellowed as she threw her sparkly pink headband at him,

"I want to be this way," Jeremy said, "It's real good. You have to join."

Vanessa continued to search for a weapon. She saw a frying pan on the stove. She grabbed it and swung it wildly.

"I have a weapon! You better be scared!" Jeremy made a grab for Vanessa, but she moved away and smacked Dollface with the frying pan. She flew across the kitchen and struck her head against the wall, causing it to fall right off!

"NOOOOOOOOOOOOOOO!" Jeremy screamed.

The torso went limp and fell to the ground. The head rolled across the limonium floor and stopped in front of Jeremy. Dollface's eyes were shut tight, her mouth was wide open. The head didn't move. Jeremy grabbed a kitchen knife from the knife tray. "You will die," he said, holding the knife, "You've been a naughty little girl,"

I'm so stupid. I could've stabbed Dollface. Vanessa thought bitterly.

Jeremy grabbed Vanessa and pinned her against the wall. His grip on her shoulders was so firm, Vanessa couldn't break free.

"You've done well, servant," Dollface said, floating next to him. "Now, finish her." Jeremy held a knife to her throat.

"Bye, bye Vanessa," Before he could cut, Vanessa remarked, "Sorry Jeremy, this just has to be done." She gathered her courage and kicked Jeremy in the groin.

"Ooooooooooh," Jeremy grunted as he fell to the floor. He sprawled in a messy heap on the floor.

"No, no, no," Dollface moaned, "You useless. I take back what I said." Jeremy laid on the ground, lifelessly.

At that moment, Vanessa heard the front door open. Stomping footsteps approached the kitchen. Her parents, along with Amy and Jamie, entered.

"What on earth is going on?" Mr. Greene asked.

"Peasants, you're here! Help me!" Dollface cried. Amy and Jamie stepped in front of Dollface. Their eyes glowed red, that same shade red, Dollface's eyes were before.

"We'll do anything you want." Amy and Jamie said at the same time. They advanced toward Vanessa. Vanessa backed away. Behind them, Jeremy had cornered Mr. and Mrs. Greene.

"Mom! Dad!"

Vanessa ripped past Amy and Jamie to help them. Jeremy smiled and held up the knife. Vanessa pushed Jeremy out of the way.

"Get out of here, Mom. I got this!" Vanessa said.

"GET HER!" Dollface commanded.

Amy and Jamie sprinted toward Vanessa. Dollface began to hover toward her.

Vanessa grabbed Dollface's head. "Let go of me, fool!" Vanessa began to squeeze the head harder and harder. "I'm warnnnning you, stop,"

"STOP, THIS AT ONCE! STOP! STOP!" Amy and Jamie cried.

Vanessa ignored them and squeezed the head harder and harder…

"Don't do thi—" The head POPPED! A cloud of pink smoke wafted the air. The smoke seemed to seep inside of Vanessa's body. In seconds, it was gone. Jeremy got up and stared dazed around the room.

"What happened?" he asked. Vanessa ran up to Jeremy and wrapped her hands around his neck, and kissed him. Jeremy put his arms on her waist and kissed her for the longest time. Then they finally stopped.

"Woah," Jeremy said.

"You, ok?" Vanessa asked.

"I-I'm fine. D-d-did the doll *possess* me?"

"Yes, but I killed her," Vanessa said.

Jeremy yawned and said, "Look, I gotta go. I'm just tired for some reason." Vanessa led him out the front door. She watched him walk down the sidewalk back home. Vanessa walked back into the kitchen to find Amy and Jamie. Their eyes were back to normal. The twins ran up to Vanessa and hugged her.

"Thank you, thank you for saving us," Amy said.

Mr. and Mrs. Greene joined in on the hug.

"You're very brave, Vanessa," Mrs. Greene said, "I love you. Even though I don't always show it. I love you."

"Thank you," Vanessa said.

Maybe, I'm not a complete screwup after all. She thought.

* * *

Saturday came, Vanessa was getting ready for that date with Jeremy. He was picking her up in a limo his dad rented. She combed her hair with trembling hands. She was nervous. Her chest felt like it could burst with excitement and nervousness.

"Vanessa, Jeremy's here!" Mrs. Greene called.

"Coming!"

Vanessa rushed downstairs and opened the front door. Jeremy stood in front of the large white limo, dressed in a tuxedo.

"Wow, you look stunning. More stunning than Lois Lane," Jeremy commented.

Vanessa laughed as she strode down the walkway in her big and poofy white dress.

"This your limo?" she said.

"Nah, my dad rented it. He's extra."

"This is gorgeous. This is my first time seeing you without that Orlando Magic Jersey."

"Don't get used to it, tuts," Jeremy said. Vanessa laughed again. Not because of what he said, but out of happiness that Dollface was gone. The chauffeur came out of the limo and opened up the door. Vanessa was about to hop in when she heard her dad yell, "Wait a minute! She spun around and saw her parents, along with Amy and Jamie.

"Listen, pal, you better have my daughter back here by six, understand," Mr. Greene said with a glare.

"Don't worry, he will. Now go." Vanessa shooed them away from the limo. Mr. Greene gave Jeremy a final disapproving look as he and Mrs. Greene went back inside the house.

"Have fun, Neth!" Jamie said.

"Hop in," Jeremy said. Vanessa started to go inside, but she felt some sort of ringing in her head. The ringing grew louder and louder, and her head started to hurt really bad.

"What's wrong, Nessa." Vanessa heard Jeremy saying. Her head hurt so badly she couldn't talk. She and Jeremy went inside the limo and sat. In Vanessa's head, she heard a clicking sound.

"Hehehehehe," She heard a chuckle inside her head. Vanessa immediately recognized it. Dollface.

"Hi, Vanessa! You thought you could get rid of me! Wrong!"

"Get out of my-" Suddenly, she couldn't talk. Vanessa opened her mouth, but no sound came out.

"No more talking. You will do what I say from now on. Do you understand?" Dollface said.

"Crystal clear, I won't let you down," Vanessa said.

"Huh?" Jeremy asked, "What are you saying?"

"Let's have some fun on this little playdate, shall we?" Dollface said and giggled.

ALIENS IN MY BACKYARD

"**A**liens are real and are on our planet right now! I'm gonna be the first one to know." I yelled at my friend, Todd.

"Uh-huh, don't kill yourself trying to find them," Todd said and laughed. I stood up and walked right up to his face.

"Storky, don't make fun of me for this. If I get rich and famous when I discover aliens. You're not getting a single dime." I often called him Storky because he was tall and had stork-like legs. He hated it, but I didn't give two fucks about it. That shit cracked me up.

"Ooh, I'm so hurt. I'm so hurt," Todd said, "I really don't give a damn."

"You will give a damn once I find them."

I was obsessed with trying to find aliens. I looked all over the neighborhood for some alien residue, some UFO parts, or some alien tapes. It had to be something that was connected to aliens.

"Well, good luck, weirdo, on your little alien hunt," Todd said and snickered. He ran down the sidewalk and quickly disappeared down the block. Todd was so naive. He obviously didn't understand what this could mean for me. I always fantasized about what I would do once I got rich and famous. First, I could buy a mansion. Second, I could get a private jet. Third, I could buy as many luxury items as I could. The private jet and the mansion were quintessential to me.

I decided to just wrap up my alien hunt for today and head back inside my home. As I turned toward my house, there was movement behind the shrubs in the front. I turned toward them, and a tall and scruffy-looking man emerged from them.

Oh shit. Is this a home intruder? How long has he been behind there?

"Hey, kid," the man whispered, "Come over here. I have something for you." I looked around me, trying to see if there were people outside. Sure enough, I saw my neighbor, Mrs. Petunia, across the street, watering her grass.

In case the man tries something. I'll scream for help, and she'll hear me.

For kicks, I decided to walk over to the man. As I got closer, I smelled shit. The man had to have pooped his pants or something.

"Hey, kid. I overheard your conversation about aliens. I've got something for you that will help you." The man dove in his pocket and pulled out a toy ray gun. Three feet long, and crimson red, the gun looked so cool. It looked just like the ones used in alien movies. My amber eyes bulged.

"Woah," I said.

"It can kill real aliens."

"Where'd you get it?"

"Don't worry about all that. Just take it."

I grabbed it.

"This conversation never happened," the creepy man said. He ran from behind the shrub and down the street.

What a weirdo. The gun looked pretty cool and all, but it was probably fake. He probably did it to just scare me. He probably stole it from some store and decided to give it to me. That man must've been some sort of crook. But it was worth trying it. I pulled the trigger on the ray gun. Nothing. No ray of light.

I knew it. It's fake. I thought.

Sighing, I went back into my house.

* * *

"Have you done your homework yet?" Mom asked as she stood in front of the television.

"No."

"Tyler Bentley, what did I tell you about these alien movies. Turn the damn movie off now. I'm not gonna keep telling you no more."

"Let me watch this scene first!" I insisted.

"Tyler." Mom's face turned serious. Her eyes burned into mine. Uh-oh, that meant that she was going to explode on me. If she did explode on me, I probably wouldn't have any of my alien movies.

"Fine, I'll do my homework."

"Wise choice."

She left my bedroom, and I paused the movie. Oh, man! I was at the climax of my favorite alien film, *Planet X.* I loved alien movies. I liked how the aliens zapped the defenseless citizens with their ray guns. Mom was right, I rarely turn in homework assignments because I watched alien movies all the time.

I put my homework on the desk, scanned through the questions, and shook my legs rapidly. I couldn't help but shake my legs. It helped me concentrate. I ran my fingers through my grubby brown mullet and looked at the first question. What is the difference between meiosis and mitosis? Don't know and don't care.

Quickly, I wrote down the answers to the homework. It didn't mean they were correct. I was in a hurry to finish watching *Planet X.* As I was about to finish, "Eek, eek, eek." The sound came from outside my window. "Eek, eek, eek." It was a faint beeping noise. I crawled up to my window and peeked out.

When I saw it, my heart sank. UFOs in the sky. Two circling UFOs over my next-door neighbor, Mr. Klein's house. *Just like the alien movies!* I blinked multiple times to assure myself that this wasn't a dream. They glowed in the dark blue sky in my backyard like stars. Quickly, I dashed to my parent's bedroom.

"What is it, Tyler?" Mom asked.

"There's a UFO in the backyard. Come look." Mom and Dad got up from their bed and followed me into my room. The sound and the UFOs were gone.

"Not funny, Tyler," Dad said, narrowing his eyes at me. He didn't like practical jokes.

"It wasn't a practical joke."

"It must've been your imagination," Mom reassured me.

"I saw them!" Mom and Dad ignored me and walked out of the room. There were UFOs. Actual aliens could've been in them. If only I had gotten a picture, they would've believed me. I'm so dumb. Why? Why didn't I do that? I stared at my homework in defeat. There was no way I was going to complete it.

* * *

My friend Todd and I walked to school. I decided to tell him about the UFOs.

"Saw UFOs in my backyard last night!"

"Yeah, right," Todd said..

"I'm fucking serious they were there."

"Uh-huh, did they take you for a ride? Aliens aren't real bozo." Todd walked past me and headed toward the school building.

"Screw you, Storky!" He turned around and gave me the middle finger. He didn't believe me.

In class, my teacher, Mrs. Juniper, started to talk about aliens. I was so into it.

"No one has ever spotted an alien before in our town," Mrs. Juniper claimed.

"But miss, Tyler said he saw UFOS last night!" Todd blurted out. Everyone in the class burst out laughing. My face turned red. I knew I was blushing.

"It's true!" I yelled. "Aliens are real! Aliens are real! They were in my backyard. They're real, I tell you, Real!"

Everyone laughed. Todd just looked at me with a sadistic smirk.

"No one has seen an alien before in this town, Mr. Bentley. I can tell you've been watching a lot of alien movies," Mrs. Juniper said sternly.

"Do you have a picture of these UFOS?" A boy called out from the back of the classroom.

"No, but I'll see the aliens again! I'll be ready for them. They'll come back! They've got to!"

Everyone laughed even harder.

"Enough, Mr. Bentley. One more outburst, or you're going to the principal's office."

I wasn't going to back down. I knew what I saw. No one was going to shut me up.

"But you guys don't understand! Aliens are real! You gotta believe me! You just have to! I'm the biggest alien expert in this—"

H! GO TO THE OFFICE!" Mrs. Juniper hollered, raising her arms in the air. I got up from my seat and walked downstairs to the principal's office. She didn't believe me either.

* * *

Principal Wartz didn't suspend me or call my parents. I got off pretty scot-free. I was fortunate but felt no remorse for what I did. Aliens had to be real, goddamnit. Later that day, I was in the living room, working on a school project. Mom and Dad were sitting on the couch, watching the six o'clock news. As I worked, I heard a news story come on about aliens.

The news reporter, Debra Weathers, explained, "There have been sightings of UFOS in Greentown." I gasped. My family and I lived in Greentown.

She added, "Also, there are five missing children from Greentown. These strange disappearances can possibly be connected to aliens."

"Oh my god!" I said. Then, a picture popped up on the screen. It showed a UFO. It looked exactly like the one I saw.

"Be careful when you're alone," Debra warned. "Aliens could take over this planet. They could've abducted these five children. We don't know how many UFOs are in our town."

The story ended.

"That story was fake," Mom commented.

"It can't be real," Dad added.

"I told you, there were UFOs in the backyard." I hollered, "They were *here!*"

"Not all news stories are real," Mom said, "That picture didn't even look like an alien."

"Yes, it did. Quit denying it, Mom!"

"This isn't up for debate, young man," Dad said.

"Aliens are here! You heard what Debra said!"

"News is full of propaganda."

"No, it's not!"

"Go to your room and don't come out for the rest of the night!"

"But Dad!"

"NOW!" Dad said, his brown eyes flashing at me. I stormed out of the living room and went to my bedroom. They were hopeless. I stormed out of the room in anger. A terrifying thought surged over me. Are aliens actually abducting kids? I saw the UFOs in my backyard last night. Maybe they were waiting to see if someone would come out of the house to seize. I walked over to my window and stared out. No UFOs. *Come on, please come back. I need to get rich.* I thought. I stared out the window for a few more hours. The UFOs never returned.

But once I got to school the next day, I found another shocking thing. Todd was not there! He was never absent! If he were going to be absent, he would tell me. I decided to go to his house after school to see if he was okay. Maybe he was sick or something.

I went straight to his house after school and got the shock of my life. The garage was wide open, revealing his parents' two Camaros. They were definitely home. I rang the doorbell and waited. After five minutes, no one answered. I pounded on the door really hard. Waited a few seconds, no one answered the door.

That's so weird. Their cars are in the garage, and yet they weren't answering the door. Confused, I pounded on the door some more. It flung open. Yes, the door flung wide open. It was unlocked. Weird. I walked in. The front hallway was dark, and it smelled like bleach.

"Hello, It's me, Tyler! Your door was open!" I didn't hear a soul in the house.

What could they possibly be doing? I wandered into the kitchen, where I was greeted with an even more pungent smell of bleach. The counters were sprayed down with it. They weren't dry. It looked as if someone just cleaned them. "Odd," I uttered. Then, I decided to look upstairs. Slowly, I walked up the stairs and went to Todd's parent's room. No one there.

"Huh?" I bellowed, breaking the silence. The bed was neatly made and the desk organized. Quickly, I went to Todd's room. He wasn't in there, nor were his parents. All of his stuff was there, as his posters and computer. His room was in disarray, with clothes strewn all over the floor. Todd's room was always messy.

Where are they? I left the room trembling and searched the entire house. I checked the bathrooms, basement, and family room. Finally, I got out of that house as fast as I could and went home. I ran inside my home, where I found Mom watering the plant in the front hall.

"Hey Tyler, what's wrong?" She asked. I ignored her and ran upstairs to my room. Mom called something after me, but I didn't hear it. I wanted to know where Todd and his family went. I tried calling his cell. It went straight to voicemail.

Where did Todd go? His parents' cars were in the garage, the door was unlocked... Did someone break in and kill them? The news story about the aliens. The five missing kids. Aliens had to have abducted Todd and his family. It sounds crazy, right? Yes, aliens abducted them. I ran downstairs to tell Mom. She was sitting on the couch, reading a book.

"Mom, Todd, and his family got abducted by aliens," I said slowly. Mom put down her book.

"For the last time, aliens aren't real, son. The story on the news was fake."

"But I went over to Todd's house. His parents' cars are in the garage. The front door was unlocked, and no one was in the house." I explained. Mom stared at me, bewildered. She didn't speak for the longest time.

"I'll call the police." Mom said, finally breaking the silence. They checked with the neighbors first. The odd circumstance caused the police to make their house a crime scene. They identified Todd and his parents as missing people.

I couldn't sleep at all last night. I waited outside my window, waiting for the UFOs to return. Todd and his family slipped into my thoughts. *What did those aliens do to them? Did they brainwash them or take them back to their planet?* I thought. Was he gone forever? So many questions and no answers. Even though they probably were abducted. I still needed to capture the aliens, report it to the government and hopefully get some money. Once I got the money, I wouldn't need friends. I could drop out of school and go somewhere far, far away.

* * *

After school, the next day, I walked home alone. It wasn't the same without Todd. We always played around together at lunch and stuff like that. When I entered my home. It was unusually quiet. Dad should've been in the living room watching TV, and Mom would prepare dinner.

It appeared that no one was home yet. They were usually here by the time I got off school. I went into the kitchen and saw the water running in the sink. I turned off the faucet, went into the living room, and noticed that the TV was on but muted.

"Mom? D-dad?" No answer.

. *Why am I so freaked out?* They could be just working late. I'll call them. I decided. I went to the phone and called Mom and Dad. But they didn't pick up their phones. It went straight to voicemail.

That's weird. I thought. Why weren't they answering the phone? Maybe they're going to come home later. I decided to go upstairs and do homework to pass the time. I hoped they would come home soon to help me with my school project.

Three hours went by. It was past six o'clock. Mom and Dad still didn't come home. I started to get a little worried. I called them again, but they didn't answer.

What's going on here? Mom and Dad should be home by now. Why didn't they call me? Why didn't they tell me this morning that they were going to be out late? I felt a shiver run down my spine. To be home alone was creepy.

Maybe Mom and Dad went to a party with some colleagues from work. That could be it. I just hoped they would come home soon. Four hours went by, Mom and Dad were *STILL* not home. It was around ten o'clock, and I had to get ready for bed. But I started pacing around the front hallway, waiting for them to walk in through the door. I even called them twenty more times, but they still didn't pick up.

I decided to just go upstairs and get ready for bed. I took a quick shower, put on pajamas, and got under the covers. But I didn't go to sleep. I kept thinking about Mom and Dad. *Did something terrible happen to Mom and Dad?* I thought. *What if... they died? No. That's crazy, Tyler. Stop with these thoughts.* I scolded myself.

Mom and Dad, where are you? Tears began to form in my eyes. Suddenly, I heard a loud noise coming from the backyard. It was a soft and familiar beeping noise. The

UFOs had returned! I crept up to the window and saw them hovering above my backyard.

A ray of light shined out of both UFOs, and two dark figures emerged. A clear image in the night, there they were. Two aliens. One had blue skin and large black eyes. The other had purple skin and humongous blue eyes. The aliens stood in front of each other.

OH MY GOD, they returned! They're in my backyard! What were they planning to do? Why have they returned to my home?

I saw their mouths move as if they were talking to each other. I opened the window so I could hear:

"Is the house empty?" The purple-skinned alien asked.

"No, we captured the mother and father, but the boy is still in there." The blue-skinned alien replied.

Mother and Father? Oh no… they captured Mom and Dad! Not my Mom and Dad! Oh no! Oh no! Now they were after me.

"How are we going to get the boy out of that house?" The purple alien said, pointing.

"We're gonna break in." The blue alien said. "Then, we'll bring him back to our planet."

Break-in? Oh no. I wasn't gonna let them capture me. I didn't know what to do. The aliens rushed over to the back door and banged on it. They're going to break down the door! I need something to stop them and fast. I searched the room to look for a weapon. But I didn't find anything that would work.

The banging continued, growing louder. They're coming for me. I thought. That's when I saw it. The ray gun. The ray gun glowed a bright yellow color in the darkroom. Slowly, I walked over to it and grabbed it. The glow stopped. I remembered the guy in the bushes saying, "It kills real aliens." Will it work this time? It was worth a try. I knew I needed to stop these aliens. No money was worth it anymore. My family and friends mattered the most.

Quickly, I grabbed it and raced downstairs. I stepped in front of the back door. I could see the two alien shadows behind the back door window. I raised the ray gun forward and tiptoed up to the door. Each step made my heart beat louder. My legs felt like Jello as if I would melt into a puddle on the floor. Slowly, I turned the knob and flung open the door.

"SURPRISE!" I yelled. I pulled the trigger, and a ray of light came out, killing the blue alien. The purple one started running across the yard.

"I request backup immediately!" The alien yelled. "Man down! Get the boy!" I raced out into the yard after the purple alien. It tried to jump the back gate to escape, but I shot it in the back.

The alien dropped to the ground. It laid there, with its eyes shut. Wow, I actually did it. I killed the aliens. The ray gun worked!

I thought it was over, but I was completely wrong. As I went into the house, I saw *five* UFOs hovering in the air towards me! They were about to crash right into me.

That's what the alien meant by the backup. I thought. I ran from the UFOs path. One of them crashed on the back porch. The other four UFOs hovered above the grass. Rays of light shone out of them, emerging the aliens. There were three pink-skinned aliens and one yellow alien holding ray guns.

"I see that you killed the Capturers," The yellow alien said, looking at the dead blue and purple aliens, "What a silly mistake."

"Now, it's up to us to kill you," A pink alien said. Then, they pointed their guns at me.

As they were about to pull the trigger, I used my ray gun and shot one of the pink aliens. It flew backward and laid down on the grass.

"Shoot him!" The yellow alien yelled. The aliens pulled their triggers. Rays of light flew towards me. I ducked down on the ground, dodging them right on time. The glow of light hit the back door, causing it to explode!

"Woah," I said. This ray gun was powerful! The yellow alien shot a ray of light towards me. I ducked and rolled out the way on time. I pulled the trigger to my gun and shot a beam towards it.

The yellow alien tried to duck, but it was too late. The ray of light hit it,

causing him to die. It laid on the ground with its arms outstretched and its mouth agape in terror. The pink-skinned aliens ran up to the dead yellow alien.

"No! He killed our emperor!" One of them said.

"We need to get out of here before the boy kills us," The other replied. "He's too

powerful!" The aliens ran back to their UFOs. They got on them and hovered up in the sky.

Oh no. I can't let them get away and possibly capture more innocent citizens. I thought. As the UFOs were about to leave, I pulled the trigger of my ray gun and shot them.

The UFOs blew up into a million pieces. A boom of fire shot up in the sky and then disappeared, killing the aliens. I did it. I knew that a ray gun could be destructive around objects.

I killed the aliens. I actually saved the world from them. I stared at the two UFOs that the blue and purple aliens left.

Maybe I can show these to someone. I thought.

"Hey!" I heard a man's voice cry out. I spun around and saw my neighbor Mr. Klein in his robe and slippers, holding a cellphone.

"I saw everything. The UFOS, the aliens, the light! Er-eh-everything!" Mr. Klein cried. "I've got it all on video,"

Mr. Klein showed the video of me fighting the aliens and all of the UFOs that flew into my backyard.

"We gotta run this to the government! This video will make us rich and famous!"

ATTACK OF THE
ROBOT COSTUME

Eddie was so complicated sometimes. One day, we're best buddies, and another day, we hate each other's guts. I still had the bruises on my face from all our fights. My face was already fucked up from all the acne on my cheeks and once baby smooth forehead. I looked like a pale-faced punk-ass freak being eaten up by soon-to-be exploding red pustules. What better person than I to host a Halloween party? Plus, My classmates and I were too old to trick or treat. John, My older brother, went to a lot of parties and he's eighteen years old. Trick or treating was for babies. I wanted to start going to parties like my brother and his friends. That's what older kids did, right? So I invited my entire class of about twenty-six to my party.

"What costumes are you guys wearing for the party?"

"I ain't tellin," Eddie said as he put his dirty bare feet on the coffee table.

"Get your dirty ass feet off the table. My mom is gonna have a cow!"

"Get your dirty ass feet off the table," Eddie mocked. He kept his feet on the table. "I'm not telling y'all what my costume is. I'm gonna surprise y'all."

I rolled my eyes.

"I'm gonna be a scientist," Keith said. "I want to be one when I grow up."

"Lame," Eddie murmured.

"But scientists are cool," Keith said. "How about you, Lloyd?"

"Don't know yet."

"Halloween is in two days. You have to hurry." Keith reminded me.

"Thanks for the reminder." I said as I rolled my eyes, "I just don't know."

"Come as yourself—Acne-man or Pizza face. You scary enough already," Eddie remarked.

"Ha-ha," I said, throwing chips at them. I haven't decided on a Halloween costume. I had a goblin costume from a couple years ago. But it was torn and old. Besides, I wore that same costume last Halloween. I wanted something different. Something scary and cool.

"My costume will be the best."

"Doubt it." Eddie said.

"Umm, We'll see."

I noticed a neighborhood newsletter on the kitchen table as I cleaned up after the guys had gone. On the front was an advertisement for a costume shop:

Costumes, Costumes and More Costumes.
Located at 19334 Cloverlane ST.
Open 9AM to 9PM

There was also a picture of the shop on the bottom. It was a small shop that had many costumes in the front window. The shop was located eight blocks from the school. Hmm, this must be new. I never heard of it before. I was excited as I thought about going there tomorrow after school.

Too bad I didn't realize that going to that store would change my life.

***

After school, I walked into town to go to the costume shop. *What costumes do they have? Do they sell scary ones?* I wondered. I passed an ice cream shop, a toy shop, and a hardware store until I finally reached the big glowing sign of the costume shop.

I went inside and immediately started shivering, and my teeth chattered because of how cold it was in there. "Hello, young man, can I help you find something?" The shopkeeper, a fat woman, greeted me. She was odd-looking with bushy brown hair, big gray eyes, and a big mole on the side of her nose. face. The most disturbing thing about her was the big creepy smile she seemed to give me.

"D-d-d-do you have any scary costumes?"

"Back of the store," She whispered while pointing. I thanked her and walked to the back. I passed rows and rows and rows of aisles. I saw all kinds of costumes: a gorilla, vampire, dog, mummy and werewolf. Too cliche. I moved to another aisle: a clown, a fox, and alien costumes. Too boring. I continued to look through the costumes. As I moved them, one fell off the hanger and to the floor. I picked it up. It was a robot but not a regular-looking robot costume. It looked spine-chilling. It was jet black with glowing red eyes that seemed to stare into my soul. Its static grin almost hid some missing teeth. It even had fake blood stains spread all over the outfit.

Yes, a unique costume.

When thinking of a scary costume, nobody thought of robots. This robot costume would make them rethink horror. It *was* so fucking scary. I put the robot costume back on the hanger and brought it to the front. The lady was reading a book, *Costume Spells.* She looked up when she heard me coming. I put the costume on the counter, but the shopkeeper held up her hand.

"Whoa, whoa, you can have the costume for free," She said, showing little emotion.

"Really? Are you sure?" I asked.

"Yes, really." She pushed the costume toward me and gave me that wide toothy, creepy smile again. It sent shivers down my spine.

"Okay, t-thanks," I said nervously. Her grin grew wider. She put the costume in a bag and handed it to me.

"I hope you enjoy the costume because you can't return it," the shopkeeper announced.

"Uh, um, what, Why not?" She ignored my question and went back to reading her book. How rude of her. I left the store. It was cloudy and super windy. The wind made the costume almost fly out of my hand. But I held tighter to it, not letting the awesome costume out of my reach. I couldn't believe I got it for free.

Anyway, I was all set for the Halloween party. Halloween night, it was party time. Mom and Dad set up a refreshments table with cookies, punch, and pizza in the basement corner. They helped me hang the streamers and lights. This was the perfect place for a party.

"All set up," Mom said as she wiped the sweat off her forehead.

"You sure we can't supervise this party," Dad said.

"I'm sure. Everything'll be fine."

"Okay, but if something gets broken, then you're not having any more parties."

"Alright, now go upstairs. My classmates will be here any minute, and I need to put my costume on."

We went upstairs, and Mom and Dad went into the living room to watch TV while I went to my room. I stared at the costume. The robot stared up at me with its chilling smile. It seemed to have grown wider. It was like the costume was enticing me to put it on. I shivered and removed the hanger, and put on the robot outfit. As soon as I put it on, the costume tightened as if it were embracing me. *Weird.*

I put on the robot head and felt that embracing feeling again. It seemed to secure my head as if the robot head was trying to replace it. The doorbell rang, and I ran downstairs to answer it. I opened the door where a tall and slender werewolf stood. The werewolf howled, staggered up to me, and playfully wrapped its right arm around my throat.

"Hey, hey. cut it out, stop," I said.

"Relax, you big baby," Eddie said. He removed the werewolf head. "Happy Halloween, punk."

"Dude, you almost gave me a heart attack."

Eddie snickered and looked me up and down. His smile turned into disgust.

"Your costume is trash," he snarled.

"Well, at least my costume isn't basic like yours," I shot back.

"Well…" Eddie paused, struggling to think of a roast. "You're just pathetic."

"Your roasting is pathetic."

"Whatever, man, where the hell the party at?"

"In the basement." I led him downstairs to the basement.

So much for what I thought was a scary costume. More kids began to arrive at around seven o'clock. The party was supposed to end at ten. Most of them hated my costume. Even my crush, Sasha, said that the costume made her want to puke. No one got the idea behind it. As I danced to the loud, blaring rap music. I felt something tap me from behind.

"Oh!"

"Hey, it's just me, Keith." I turned around and saw Keith in his scientist costume. He wore a white lab coat, goggles, and big black gloves.

"Oh hey, you liking the party?" I said.

Keith nodded. "That robot costume is just excellent," He said.

"Thanks, I got it from a new costume shop," *At least somebody likes my costume!*

"What's the store called?" Keith asked.

"Costumes, Costumes, and More Costumes."

We danced for a little bit and ate pizza and cookies. An hour went by. While we danced, some kids goofed around by the refreshment table and pushed a tray of cookies off the table. "Oh no," A boy in a Teletubbies Costume said sheepishly. I stopped the music, and everybody looked at the crushed cookies on the floor.

"I'll... go... get... a...broom," I said in a robotic voice. Wait? Huh? What happened to my voice?

I went upstairs and passed the living room where Mom and Dad were watching a movie. They had big bowls of popcorn in their hands.

"What do you need, Lloyd?" Mom asked.

"I, am, going, to, go, get, a, broom." There it was again, my voice sounded just like a...robot.

"Why are you talking like that?" Dad demanded, getting up from the couch.

"It is just acting."

"You really sound like a robot," Mom said. I thanked her and quickly got the broom. I went back to the basement and swept up the cookies on the floor. *Why do I sound like a robot? Was it something I ate or drank? It had to be, right?*

At that moment, I started to feel weird. My vision became blurry, everything started to turn blue. I took the dustpan and broom back upstairs. "Woah," I said. I almost slipped on a step. I plodded back upstairs. My arms and legs swung in front of me.

Why am I walking so strangely? I tried to walk normally, but I kept moving rigidly. I managed to put the broom and dustpan back into the kitchen then scuffled out of there. I didn't know what was happening to me. I trudged back to the party, where I ran into Keith.

"Don't you want to take off that robot head?" he asked, "You must be sweating like a pig."

"Oh yeah, great idea."

I put my hands at the bottom of the robot head and pried it up. "Ouch," I said. My hands hit a block of metal. There was no bottom to the head which made the terrifying truth hit me. I *had* become a robot. The robot costume was *alive*.

"Keith, I am a robot," I said in a robotic voice.

"Hahaha, very funny," Keith said. "What a stupid joke."

"I am serious." Keith just laughed and laughed at me until he couldn't breathe. Tears of joy had filled his eyes. He wasn't taking me seriously. Some friend he was!

"It's not empirically possible. You can't just turn into a robot. There's no science behind that whatsoever."

"Oh, you're useless." I moved away from him.

Maybe Eddie would believe me. I shuffled across the basement and scanned among the costumes. Finally, I saw him talking to a girl dressed as Cat-Woman. Quickly, I rocked myself over to him.

"Eddie, Eddie, My, costume, is, alive, You, have, got, to, help, me."

"Not now, Lloyd, I'm making my move."

"This, is, important, please, help."

Eddie glared at me, then turned to the girl and said, "I'll talk to you later." She walked off and went back to the group of wallflowers hanging out in the basement corner.

"What's your fucking deal, man? Why'd you embarrass me like that? Huh?" Eddie asked. His blue eyes were piercing me with anger.

"But,the,costume,is,alive." I said.

"Why are you talking like a robot, dude? Quit fucking playing with me."

"It,is,the, costume" I said.

"Ugh, get the fuck away from me. I got you on sight, Monday. Prepare to get your tenth ass whooping from me this year." I trotted away from him. There was no talking it through now. I couldn't believe neither Keith nor Eddie would fucking hear me out that the costume was fucking alive.

The robot costume was actually alive. The shopkeeper had to have some strange powers or something. I remembered the title of the book she was reading, *Costume Spells*. She must've cast a spell on this costume. I rocked out of the basement and shuffled through the living room. I was headed out the front door, but Mom stopped me.

"Where are you going? The party's still going." She said.

"The robot costume is alive," I said. I shuffled out the front door. Mom yelled something after me, but I didn't hear it. I lumbered along like a lunatic out in the night. I plodded past a group of trick-or-treaters, and some stopped to look at and compliment me on my costume. Many adults gave me dirty looks.

They must think I'm crazy. But maybe I am. As I shuffled, I took a wrong step and tripped. I fell to the ground hard, and I smashed my metalhead on the floor.

"Ow," I moaned. I laid on the ground for a second. Eventually, I brought myself to my feet and staggered forward. Finally, I reached town. The town was practically empty. It was like a ghost town. I didn't see the car. The next thing I knew, the vehicle rammed into me. Bam! I felt my whole life flash before my eyes. I remembered my family vacation to Chicago last year. I remembered the concerts that Keith and I went to. I remembered the fights Eddie and I had. I always lost them and came home with many cuts and bruises. All of those scenes yet fond and bad were all flashing at me so fast that I couldn't comprehend them. All the way from birth and up until the very moment the party started.

I fell backward and hit my head on the cement. The car swerved past me and sped off, going about one hundred miles in an hour. *Is that driver drunk or what?* I laid sprawled on the ground, staring up at the dark sky. *I can't get up. I can't move a muscle. I just can't do it.* I was defeated. Couldn't go on anymore. *No. No. No. Lloyd, you must go on. You have to confront the shopkeeper.*

With my limited energy, I tried to stand up but couldn't. *I'll just crawl.* I brought myself up to a crawling position and began to crawl. Slowly, I shuffled past the shops. My arms trembled, and they felt like noodles. I almost broke out of the crawling position. If I did, I definitely wasn't going to get back up. Finally, I saw the sign for the costume shop in the distance, about six feet away.

Almost there, Lloyd. You got this. I gathered speed. Getting closer and closer to the shop. Closer and closer. I was a couple feet from it now. *Onward. Don't give out now. Please,*

God, don't make my noodle arms give out. Finally, I got to the door and peered up.

A sign on the front door said: **OUT OF BUSINESS**. Oh, fuck no. I peered inside the front window through my red eyes. I gasped. There were no costumes, no racks, no shopkeeper, nothing.

I guess being a robot is a new normal for me now. Hey, at least I can get programmed to do things without doing them myself. It'll be awesome. What's more awesome is that no one will ever see my bad acne again. Plus, I won't have to fight Eddie on Monday.

WEEKEND AT GREEN LAKE

I was prepared to have the worst weekend of my life. No, really, this was going to be the worst weekend of my fucking life. All thanks to Mom and Dad. We were going to be staying in a disgusting log cabin that overlooks the lake. I wasn't an outdoors person. I hated mosquitos, grass, and anything that was outside, really. I was hoping my parents would change their minds about the lake. Nope. There we were on Friday, putting bags in the trunk of Dad's SUV. I already had plans to go to Jump Park with my friends this weekend.

"Why do we have to go to the lake?" I whined while getting inside the SUV.

"Samantha, we've been over this," Mom snapped. "We're going to be doing some family bonding. We don't get to do that a lot."

Mom and Dad were doctors, and they worked all day, even on weekends. They were rarely home. Of all the places we could've gone, they chose the stupid lake. I kicked the back of the passenger seat in frustration.

"Samantha, stop it. You're fifteen years old. Act like it!" Mom hollered. Dad finished putting the bags in the trunk and got in the driver's seat. Out of the driveway and onto the lake. Dad drove for what seemed like hours until we came into a tree-filled area. We went by oak and sassafras trees. I finally saw the sign, 'Green Lake'.

Why is it called Green Lake? I wondered. *Is the lake actually green?* There was no way I was going to swim in that water. There could be all sorts of disgusting vermin, scum, protozoa, creatures, and bacterial eating fish swimming around it. We received the key to the cabin and drove to it. Once we reached it, I saw the lake. My prediction about it being green was true. I was able to see it through the car window. There was also a dock on the lake where some ducks were standing. Probably waiting to be fed. We got out of the car.

Dad took the bags from the trunk. I grabbed my small duffel bag and walked up to the cabin. The log cabin was small and still. Mom unlocked it, and we went inside. We were immediately hit by a wave of heat inside the cabin. Promptly, I started sweating.

"Guess we have to turn on the AC," Dad murmured, fanning himself. We came into the living room, which had an oversized couch and a prehistoric box TV. In the kitchen, there was a small oven, counter, and microwave. I followed Mom and Dad upstairs. The bathroom was behind the door in the front to the left at the top of the stairs. I entered a bedroom with one bed, shaggy carpet, a dresser, and a closet.

"This is our room," Dad said.

"Am I supposed to sleep on the couch?" I asked. They both nodded. Ugh, the couch didn't look comfortable at all. I walked back downstairs and set my bag down. I turned on the TV, no cable, and there was a commercial about the flu.

"Samantha, turn that TV off and go explore the lake," Mom said as she walked downstairs.

"Mom, this place sucks," I complained.

"You haven't seen a thing. Now go. I'll have dinner ready in an hour." Reluctantly, I shut the TV off and stormed out of the cabin in frustration. As soon as I got outside, a mosquito bit me in the arm.

"Ow." I slapped it away. I hated this place. There was nothing to do here. I walked to the lake and saw two men paddling a canoe. I heard one of the men say something, and the other laughed. At least they seemed to be having a good time.

"Hello," a voice said from behind me. I spun around in horror and faced a boy around my age. There was something weird about him. He didn't look like any teenage boy I've ever seen. Maybe it was the pair of brown eyeglasses on his head along with white glasses he wore over his gray eyes. Perhaps it was his inside-out yellow T-shirt. Or maybe it was the macaroni necklace he wore around his long and slender neck. The boy also held a perfume bottle in his hand.

Who the fuck is this weird-looking kid.

"Why'd you scare me like that," I demanded.

"Oh, I didn't mean to. I'm so very sorry. Jeff Bean is the name."

"Samantha Gold."

"Samantha Gold, why are you here?" Jeff asked.

"My family forced me. We're here for the weekend." I said. "This is our cabin." I pointed to it. Jeff looked at me. His periwinkle-colored eyes burned into mine. It was as if he was staring into my soul, trying to figure me out.

"Where's your cabin?" I asked.

"Over there." He pointed to a small cabin in the far distance. "I'm here to see the zombies."

"Excuse me?" Did he say the *zombies?*

"You don't know the story of the Green Lake zombies?"

I shook my head.

"About four years ago, a group of five teenagers were on a canoe…" Jeff began in a low voice.

"But the canoe flipped over, and they drowned. They didn't know how to swim. No one could hear them scream, so they went down… down to the bottom of the lake."

I sneered at him. Jeff continued his story.

"It's rumored that they turned into disgusting… decomposing… zombies," Jeff said.

I burst out laughing. I laughed and laughed until I couldn't breathe. "What's wrong with you? Zombies aren't real. You've watched too many horror movies," I said.

"I don't watch horror movies."

"Whatever, man."

Who was this moron? The only zombie I saw was him. Zombies don't exist. It had to be a fake story he made up to try to scare me. "You're ridiculous," I said, bending forward-looking him in the eye.

"I'm going to use this special concoction my mother made, Terrent. It scares creatures away. I want the zombies off this lake." Jeff held up the glass spray bottle. It had a blue liquid inside of it. He sprayed it. Surprisingly, the smell smelled sweet, like carnations.

I laughed again. "You're stupid."

"Make fun of me all you want. You're gonna fall into the hands of the undead," Jeff said.

"I can perfectly handle myself, thanks."

Jeff tsk-tsked, "I don't know."

"How the fuck you gonna find these fake zombies, weirdo."

"I can detect their vibes. They're evil vibes, like, like really beyond bad." Jeff said. "I can sense them right now." A gust of wind blew his long silver hair.

"How can you detect their presence."

"I can detect energy, Samantha Gold. You seem to have a lot of negative energy around you." Jeff began to sniff the air. "Yep, this is definitely negative energy. I know you're not happy about this place. I understand. Do you care to talk about it?"

Is this kid for real? No, I'm not gonna tell you about it, crazy.

"H-how did you know that."

"My mommy taught me everything about detecting energy."

"Yeah right."

Jeff laughed and said, "What a naive girl. Don't come crying to me when a zombie bites your head off," He turned and walked back to his cabin.

Yeah, and how would I look for him without a head. I just couldn't help but laugh. He was just a weird kid, making up stories and pretending to detect energy to fight his boredom. That did it for me. I decided to go back to my cabin and not explore the lake.

* * *

I slept on the couch that night. I tossed and turned, trying to get comfortable, but I couldn't. The sofa was so stiff.

Come on, Samantha, go to sleep. I thought unhappily. It was quiet in the cabin. So slow that you could hear a pin drop on the floor. As I was about to doze off, I listened to a splash in the lake, breaking the night silence.

I sat upright, only allowing my eyes to move. *Who on earth would be swimming in the lake right now?* I heard splashes again. They were much louder and had aggressive splashes. My curiosity got the better of me. I wanted to see who it was.

I got up from the couch and tipped-toed up to the front window. I peered through the blinds, but there was no one.

The splashing stopped, but I saw moving ripples in the water. It seemed like whoever it was just left. *Who was at the lake just now?* I wondered. Weird. I shrugged it off and went back to bed.

Saturday morning after breakfast, there was a knock on the cabin door. I opened it, and it was Jeff. Today, he had his silver hair wrapped in a messy ponytail along with red eyeglasses on his head. He wore green eyeglasses over his eyes today. Jeff also held the Terrent in his right hand.

"Wanna go for a walk?" he asked, "It's beautiful out."

"Sure, I guess." We walked on a trail that went into the trees. Jeff was right. It was a beautiful sunny day without a cloud in the sky. We continued to walk on the trail. I noticed Jeff wasn't wearing any shoes.

"Where are your shoes?"

"I love being barefoot on long walks. I like how the grass and the dirt feels on my feet. It's like a free foot pedicure."

"Oh,"

At last, we came into the woods.

"Oh no!" Jeff cried, stopping dead in his tracks.

"What's wrong?" I asked.

Jeff pointed to a tall oak tree that was covered in green moss.

"T-that tree is covered in moss. Oh no. Oh no. It's not good! It's not good, Samantha Gold. My mom used to say that trees covered in moss mean something bad has happened."

"Jeff, that's so ludicrous. It's not true."

"It's true. I'm detecting bad vibes in this area right now. We must be careful." Jeff said as he sprayed the Terrent concoction. We continued to move along the trail. I saw blue jays and robins flying around trees.

"I wish my mom were here. She could protect me. She's made some quite unique potions. My mommy is a brilliant potion maker."

"She is?"

Jeff nodded. "She spent many hours down in her lab. Barely spent time with the family. Her free time was mostly spent on me, teaching me her beliefs. Daddy couldn't take it anymore and just divorced her and took me with him to a new home."

"I'm so sorry to hear that."

"It's all good though, I've got my dad. He's ok." Jeff said.

We continued to walk along the trail.

"Sam, look at that!" Jeff yelled out suddenly. He pointed at something up ahead. I stopped dead in my tracks and stared in his direction. What I saw made me almost vomit my guts. There was a dead deer, but it was cut open. The deer had been disemboweled. There was a pool of thick blood beside it.

"Oh my god!" Jeff exclaimed.

"It must've been some sort of wild animal."

"No, it was a zombie. They eat humans and animal flesh."

"But zombies aren't real, it cou—" I stopped. Jeff had a look of panic. His eyes darted around so much that I thought they would fall out of his head.

"The zombies are here, and they're going to kill us next," he cried. "Oh, I knew it. I knew that something bad happened here. I knew it!" Jeff started running back towards the lake.

"Jeff! Jeff!" He was gone. Out of sight. Why was he so freaked out? Zombies aren't real. Plus, he knew that he was full of shit about being able to detect bad vibes. At dinner, I confessed what happened. "Jeff and I saw a dead deer today on our walk!" I said at dinner. Mom and Dad dropped their forks. Mom narrowed her eyes at me.

"A deer?" she asked.

"It was so disgusting. It was torn apart!"

"It had to be a coyote or something that killed it," Dad said, "Coyotes are pretty common in this area."

"It could be." It made perfect sense. That had to be it. It was nothing to freak out over. But what happened that night made me think otherwise. I was on the couch, again struggling to fall asleep. Then I heard the splashing sounds again. They were loud and aggressive splashes. Someone was playing in the lake. This was not my imagination this time. I was wide awake and alert. So I crept out of bed to the window. I peered through the blinds and almost screamed. A reclining figure floated up out of the water onto the dock. The person then assumed a menacing stance. I watched the figure walk off the dock. Eerily, it staggered toward our cabin.

Oh my goodness. I couldn't believe it. The moonlight reflected off of the decomposing zombie. It had a rotten face with dangling worms, tattered clothes, and pale decaying skin. The zombie flashed its teeth, revealing ugly black teeth. Steadily, it strode its way over to the front door, staring at it. The zombie had a confused expression as if it'd never seen a door before.

I couldn't believe it. My mouth dropped open in horror. The zombies were real! Suddenly, the zombie started to jiggle the handle on the front door. It's *going to break in.* I thought. "Mom, Dad!" I ran upstairs to their bedroom. "Mom, Dad!" I shook them awake. They woke up with very annoyed expressions on their faces.

"Samantha, what on earth are you doing in here?" Mom demanded.

"There's a zombie downstairs."

"A zombie?" Dad asked.

"Yes, it's trying to get in the house."

"Samantha, please, it's almost three a.m,"

"Listen to me, there's a zombie. Come look!" I insisted. I tried to shove them out of bed. Mom and Dad followed me downstairs. They opened up the front door, but the zombie was gone.

"There was a zombie," I said. "I heard it come out of the lake and come to the door."

"Samantha, I know what you're trying to pull," Dad said, narrowing his eyes. "You made up this zombie story so we can leave."

"No, I'm serious."

"Go back to bed, Samantha and don't bother us anymore tonight." Mom said coldly.

That was how it ended. Mom and Dad thought I was a wack-job. But I was sure Jeff would believe me. It was all over.

* * *

After breakfast the next day, I went over to Jeff's cabin to talk about the zombie. It was a nice cloudy day, and the wind made my long hair blow. Finally, Jeff came to the door barefoot, with his silver hair down to his shoulders. He wore big pink sunglasses without the lenses.

"What's up, Samantha Gold?" He greeted me.

"Wanna go for a walk?" He nodded, and we went off.

"I detected some really, really bad energy last night! I couldn't sleep." Jeff said.

"What happened?"

"So I went outside and…and…and."

"Spit it out," I demanded.

"I saw a zombie. It was so… angry and disgusting. I… I tried to use Terrent to get rid of it, but it wouldn't go away. So I ran back inside my house, and the zombie almost came in. I saw its eyes. It's angry eyes. It wanted to kill me. It wanted to…"

Jeff burst into tears. I put my arm on his shoulder.

"I managed to shut the door and run upstairs to tell my dad. He didn't believe me." Jeff whimpered.

"Same with me. I saw a zombie coming out of the lake. It was so disgusting and—" Jeff cut me off. But before I could continue speaking, a voice from behind us called out, "Hey, Jeff!" We spun around and saw a tall, robust man. He had curly brown hair with glasses.

"Want to go fishing with me, Jeff." The man asked.

"This is my dad."

"Oh."

He looks nothing like you. He actually looks normal.

"I don't want to go fishing. There are zombies in the lake." Jeff declared.

"Nonsense, there's nothing in there," Mr. Bean said, "I bet you're saying this to get out of father-son bonding time."

"Fine," Jeff said and sighed. "I'm getting bad vibes from doing this, though. They're literally in the air. I can smell them."

"You're just like your mother. Into that hocus-pocus shit. I was hoping this was just a phase."

"This is all I have left of my mother. She taught me everything about detecting energy. I don't know why you can't understand that."

"I'm not gonna argue with you right now. Not in front of your girlfriend." Mr. Bean said, looking at me.

"She's not my girlfriend, daddy."

"Can you stop calling me daddy and just call me Dad like a normal person, please."

"Whatever, daddy."

Mr. Bean looked at me.

"Who's this lovely girl, then?"

"I'm Samantha," I said.

"Are you with your parents in that cabin?" Mr. Bean asked, pointing to my cabin the far distance.

I nodded.

"Good, good, good. You and your parents should come with us." he said, beaming. I knew there were zombies in the water. But I didn't want to hurt his feelings and not go fishing.

Reluctantly, I said, "Sure."

"Great," Mr. Bean beamed.

"She doesn't want to come, Dad. She's lying to you. I can tell," Jeff said.

"Be quiet, boy. This'll be fun."

He walked back with us to my cabin. I told Mom and Dad about the fishing trip and they were thrilled. We all came back to his cabin and gave fishing rods to all of us.

"We're going to go fishing in that beauty," Mr. Bean said while pointing to a small white boat.

"Nice," Dad said. We all crammed inside the boat. I was hoping we kept the boat closer to the shore in case the zombies got us.

"Can you keep the boat closer to the shore?" I asked. "The zombies will eat us."

"Samantha, stop it with the zombie crap." Mom snapped.

"I'm detecting bad energy. It's so bad. We need to get off the boat."

"Be quiet, Jeff. You're not getting out of this." Mr. Bean snapped.

"There are bad vibes in this lake. Bad things. Really bad. There's evil in this lake. Something terrible is going to—"

"THATS ENOUGH!" Mr. Bean shouted. "You're going fishing, and that's final. You're not just gonna lay on your butt inside the cabin."

Jeff shrugged and said, "I still think something bad is going to happen."

"Weird kid," Dad muttered to Mom. She nodded her head. I didn't think he was being. Jeff was actually right. There was danger in that lake. We couldn't get out of the fishing trip, though. Jeff and I were roped into this.

Mr. Bean turned on the engine on the boat, and it moved towards the lake's center. He gave us worms to use as bait for the fish. I hated fishing. I didn't like the waiting aspect of it. We all threw our fishing lines in the water.

"I don't know about this. I'm getting horrible signals," Jeff warned.

"I hope I catch a bass," Dad said. I waited for a few minutes until I felt a tug on my rod.

"I got something." I reeled in the object. But the rod felt heavy. It didn't feel right. I just had a feeling. I felt like I wasn't reeling in a fish.

I couldn't reel the object in. It was too weighty. I looked in the water and screamed. There was a face in the water. A decomposing zombie face. Before I could move, it launched up from the water and grabbed the side of the boat tightly.

"AHHHHHHHHHHHHHHHHHHHHHHHHHHHHHH!" We all screamed. Looks of horror fell over us.

"DRIVE THE BOAT BACK TO SHORE!" I yelled at Mr. Bean. Quickly, he steered the boat back around. I looked back and saw five zombies swimming in the lake, trying to catch up. We got the boat back to the shore and sprinted out of it quickly. The zombies had caught up to us. They emerged from the water and stood upright, flashing us angry grimaces.

"Run!" Mr. Bean yelled. We ran back to the cabin. The zombies straggled behind us. Their faces were more wasted than ever. The skin was starting to peel from their bodies.

"I'll save us!" Jeff cried. He took out the glass bottle full of Terrent. He opened up the cork lid and threw the whole bottle at the zombies.

"Begone, bad energy! Begone! Get a taste of Terrent! Get these foul creatures out of here!"

It didn't seem to faze the zombies. They just lumbered even closer.

"Wait, why isn't it working? Why isn't it working?"

I ran back over to Jeff and shouted, "MOVE YOUR ASS! COME ON!" But as Jeff was about to run. The zombies already had him. One of the zombies bit him in the neck.

"Samantha," That was Jeff's last word before he transformed. His skin turned an ugly green color. Not a bright green but a green that would make someone want to throw up. Jeff's silver hair fell out and left him with a bald head. His glasses fell off his face to the ground. A zombie stepped on the glasses, breaking them into pieces. His eyes fell out of their sockets and left empty and deep holes.

"NO!!!!!" I shouted. Not Jeff. Oh no! No!

"NO!!! W-w-w-why!"

"Samantha, we gotta go!" Mom shouted from the cabin. "He's gone. He's one of them now." I had no other choice but to go. I ran back to the cabin with the zombies in high pursuit, chasing me. Dad opened up the cabin door for me, and I burst inside. Mr. Bean shut the door quickly, but the zombies were already there, banging loudly, letting out choked gasps.

"Did my son just die out there?" Mr. Bean said, coming up to me. His beady gray eyes locked on me. "WAS THAT MY SON?" He started shaking me hard.

"Yes," I said, sobbing. Tears were rolling down my cheeks.

Fucking fantastic," Mr. Bean muttered, walking away from me. He started pacing up and down the cabin.

"How could you let this happen?"

"It wasn't my fault!"

"Calm down, Bill," Dad said.

"Calm down? My son just died, goddamnit." Mr. Bean shouted as he burst into tears.

"Ummm, guys, What are we going to do about them?" Mom asked, pointing to the window. We looked in her direction and saw zombies banging on the window. One successfully managed to pound a hole in the glass and stick its hand inside.

"We gotta find a weapon," I declared.

"I really don't care anymore. The zombies can come and take me for all I fucking care." Mr. Bean whimpered.

"No, they're not gonna take you. You have to man up and fight." I ran around the cabin, searching for a weapon. Mom and Dad stood at the window, trying to keep the zombies from coming in through there. I ran into the kitchen, flung open all the drawers until I found big kitchen knives.

"Oh no, they're coming in," Mom shrieked. "We can't hold them much longer!"

"I got some knives!"

As I was about to run over to help Mom and Dad. Two of the zombies pounded giant manholes into the door. Mr. Bean was standing right in front of the door. Before he could move, the zombies wrapped their arms around his throat. They brought him closer and pinned him up against the door.

"Mr. Bean! I'm coming!"

"Don't! It's my time to go. I need to see Jeff. It's about time I come to see him."

After saying that, one of the zombies bit him in the neck. Blood spurted out like a water hose and landed on me. His skin turned green, and his eyes fell right out of their sockets. The zombies let go of him and Mr. Bean began to stagger towards me. Quickly, I raised the big butcher knife and stabbed him in the chest.

"Uh," Mr. Bean, the zombie, held his chest, trying to stop the blood from coming out. He held out his hand and collapsed on the floor. He laid there, not moving. "FUCK!" I yelled. I ran up to Mom and Dad and pushed them out of the way. I stabbed a zombie in the face, and it began to run away from the window,

Quickly, I went back into the kitchen for more weapons. I flung open the cabinets under the sink and found pots and pans.

"Use these as weapons," I shouted. Mom and Dad rushed over to me and grabbed pots and pans from the kitchen.

"Let's kill em," Dad said. We all dashed outside. Two zombies staggered toward us. I smacked one with a large frying pan. It fell to the ground with a hard thud. Mom and Dad hit the other zombie with giant pots. The two zombies laid on the ground. They didn't move. Their eyes were shut.

"Hey, I think we killed them," I said. But I was wrong. The zombie got back up. They were angrier than ever. Their eyes charged on Mom. One of the zombies grabbed Mom and pushed her down to the ground.

"Get off of me!" she cried. Dad and I rushed over to help her. Simultaneously, we hit the zombie away with our pots and pans. The zombie fell to the ground. It let out loud choked gasps as it stared up at the sky. Suddenly, it started to get brighter outside. I looked up at the sky and saw the sun was coming out. The zombies stumbled away from us and shielded their eyes. They let out loud hissing noises.

"They don't like the sunlight," Mom observed. One of the zombies POPPED like a balloon. Then another. The remaining zombies started running towards the tall trees in the woods. But they were too late. One of them popped. Then another. And then the last one. All of the zombies were gone. We were safe.

"T-t-that was…..intense," Dad stammered.

"No kidding." I declared, slapping him a high five.

"I'm glad we're safe from those horrible creatures." Mom said.

Later, we packed our bags and left the cabin. We put the bags in the car and left the lake. I was glad that we never had to come back there. I was never going swimming or fishing ever again! But I knew I was going to miss Jeff. Jeff was a fighter, he died trying to save us, and we all thought he was silly. Jeff was up in heaven now with his father. Halfway through our trip back home, I noticed Mom kept rubbing her neck.

"Ow. Ow. Ow." she said.

"Mom, what's wrong?"

"I think one of those zombies bit me in the neck." My mouth dropped open. I saw a red bite mark on the side of her neck. Suddenly, Mom began to change. Her skin turned into a scaly green. Her face changed into a disgusting decayed face. Her clothes ripped off her body. She became a disgusting ZOMBIE!

THE WISHING STICK

"**G**ive me back my comic book!" Austin shouted. Everyone was watching the boys outside in front of the school. School was over, and kids were beginning to leave, but they stopped to watch us.

"What are you going to do about it, wimpy?" Austin's bully Jonathan growled. He raised the comic book higher in the air. Austin jumped up—trying to grab it, but he kept lifting it higher. Austin was short at only four foot ten. Johnathan was six feet tall. "You're such a weakling," Jonathan snarled.

He started laughing like a hyena. Everyone else started laughing too. More kids walked out of the school, and they stayed and watched them. All of them were gathered in a big circle around them. Some of them had their phones held up, getting ready to record, itching for something juicy to happen.

"Whatcha' gonna do, weakling, whatcha gonna do? What's this weak ass motherfucker gonna do?" Johnathan taunted.

Austin was so sick of Johnathan's bullying. *Five months of torture, embarrassment, and harassment were about to come to an end. I needed that fucking comic book back. This ends now.* Austin raised a fist and gave Johnathan a punch in the stomach. It didn't seem to hurt him at all.

"Nice try," Jonathan said nastily. Everyone started oohing.

"You gon' let that piece of shit hit you like that," Jonathan's little friend, Chuck Barrels, said. He was the complete opposite of Johnathan in terms of height. Chuck was a midget and was morbidly obese. The Mario Bros shirt he had on looked so tight that shit looked like it might explode off his back at any given moment.

"Teach him a lesson," Suzie Barns said. She was Johnathan's girlfriend. Her physique was similar to Johnathan's. She had big bulging muscles and wore her hair in two braids. Her nose was big and seemed to match a large forehead. People often thought she looked more like a man.

"This is how you punch," Jonathan raised a fist and punched Austin hard in the face. Austin fell to the ground with a hard THUD. But he wasn't done yet. He threw himself on top of him and pinned him down to the ground. All of the flashing lights from their phone cameras were on. Kids shouted chants.

"Get him, Johnathan!"

"No mercy!"

"Don't let Austin win!" The loud chants from everybody almost felt very distant as Johnathan started punching Austin in the face hard. Wham! Wham! He could taste blood in his mouth and his teeth loosening out of place.

"WORLDSTARRRRRR!" Austin heard a kid yell.

Austin felt blood trickling out of his nose. The cheers sounded even further away. Everything felt muddled. There were sharp shades of red, then black and the stars, the stars circling. Everything after that was a daze. He had been knocked out cold. He didn't know how long he was out. One of the kids got the principal, and he brought Austin to the nurse. The nurse gave him an ice pack. The principal called his mom, and she picked him up.

"I can't believe you got into a fight with that boy," Mrs. Shep complained as she drove.

"Mom, he took my comic book," Austin protested. When he said each word, his mouth hurt from the punches.

"You fight over a damn comic book? You're at school fighting for *that*?"

"He's been fighting me since the beginning of the school year. I was tired of him messing with me, so I got even." Austin continued.

"I don't wanna hear any of that. You need to just ignore him and do your work. Maybe if you did your damn schoolwork, he wouldn't have the time to mess with you." Mrs. Shep said.

How? He'd still find time to mess with me.

"B-but." Austin stuttered.

"Sit back. Your dad and I are going to settle on your punishment once we get home."

Mrs. Shep continued driving home in silence. Of course, when Austin got home, She and his father punished him for two weeks, all thanks to Jonathan. That night, Austin was about to go to bed. As he got under the covers, he felt something crawly, squishy and cold on his legs. His legs turned to ice.

"EEEKKKKK!" Austin jumped out of bed. The blankets fell to the floor as he turned on the bedside table lamp. On the sheets, there were slimy and long purple worms. Hundreds of them wiggling on my sheets.

"Ewwwww," Austin groaned. He heard cackling from the doorway. He turned around and saw his bratty, ten-year-old sister Paula. From the look on her face, he knew she did it. *Of course, she put the worms in my bed. She liked to play all kinds of practical jokes on me.*

"Why'd you put worms in my bed?" Austin asked, with his hands on his hips.

"Scared you," she teased. She cackled even louder. Austin threw a pillow at her. Paula flashed him an angry look and left the room.

"What a scaredy-cat," she muttered as she disappeared down the hall.

Oh great, now I have to clean up the worms. Austin managed to take the worms off my sheet and throw them back outside. He changed the sheets and went back to bed. Still, Austin felt that prickly, crawling feeling on my leg, though. He had such a terrible day. Heck, every day was awful, thanks to Johnathan and Paula. *I wished for a change. Something that will give me power over them. Something that will make them pay for all the hell they put me through. I needed revenge. Revenge, such a beautiful word.* Finally, Austin slept a deep and dreamless sleep.

The next day, as Austin walked to school, He knew everyone wouldn't let him live down the fight he had with Johnathan. Especially Jonathan. He probably wanted to beat him up again, but with his minions Steve and Suzie to help finish the job.

Bam!

"Oof!" They both hit the ground hard. Austin didn't see the lady. Her purse fell to the ground.

"I'm so sorry," Austin said while helping her up. The woman had gray hair, olive-green eyes, and dressed in all black clothing. She calmly said, "It's fine, dear." She picked up her purse and gave me a forced warm smile.

"I'm sorry," Austin repeated.

"No worries. Thank you for helping, my dear. I must repay you for your kindness." The woman said. Her eyes flashed into his.

"You don't have to give me anything."

"Oh, I insist," The woman rummaged through her purse. She pulled out a golden stick with a ball on the end of it. "This is a wishing stick. Only use it for good," she said, handing him the stick.

"Thanks," Austin's voice trembled. The lady gave him a slight nod and walked away. Austin examined the stick. *Wishes. Was the lady some kind of loon? Is she totally crazy?* All of a sudden, someone grabbed the stick from Austin's hand. He turned around and saw the revolting giant. Jonathan lumbered over him with a big hungry grin on his face.

"Give it back."

"Take it." He raised it higher. Austin jumped but couldn't reach.

"Ugh, I wish you were small," he complained. Then, the golden ball at the end of the stick glowed a blood-red color. Jonathan began to shrink and shrink. Until he was about three feet tall. Austin stared in amazement. *Woah, the stick really does work.*

"Y-y-you're a wizard," Johnathan stammered. Austin grabbed the stick from the ground and put it in my backpack. He was taller than him.

"It's payback time, bud," Austin said as he cracked his knuckles. He walked closer to Johnathan and smacked him in the face. Johnathan stumbled backward and fell to the ground.

"OWWWWWWWWWWWWWW!" he howled.

"See ya," Austin waved at him and left. Jonathan stood there with his swollen cheek. Austin continued walking to school. He couldn't believe it. *The stick grants wishes. The lady must have some strange powers. School is going to be fun today.*

* * *

"Ok, class, put everything away," Austin's history teacher, Mrs. Abraham, said. "It's time for our World War II quiz." Everybody started putting things under their desks. The pop quiz. Austin had forgotten to cram yesterday. Mrs. Abraham gave everyone a quiz and went back to her desk. Everyone took the quiz. Austin looked at all eighteen multiple-choice questions.

What year did the war start? Who fought in the war? He didn't have a clue. Out of the corner of Austin's eye, he spotted the wishing stick poking out of his backpack. An idea came to him. He looked up at Mrs. Abraham's desk. She was on her computer, typing away fast.

Austin grabbed the stick from his bag with trembling hands, almost dropping it. "I wish for all the answers to the quiz," he whispered. The ball on the end of the stick glowed red. Then, the answers were circled. *Yes,* he thought. All of the responses were bubbled in on the test. Kids started to turn in their quizzes to Mrs. Abraham. Austin brought his up with a big smile. I'm *finally going to get an "A." It'll be my first one of the school year.*

Lunchtime came, and the lunchroom was as noisy as ever. Kids yelling and eating their food. Austin saw a group of boys having a mini food fight at the end of the lunchroom. Austin went over to the hot lunch line and saw that it was really long. *So long it went out the cafeteria door. I don't feel like waiting. By the looks of the line, we'll be here till the end of the period.* He thought. Austin held up the wishing stick and said, "I wish for everyone to freeze," The red ball glowed, and everyone froze. "Sweet."

Austin pushed past people in line and went into the kitchen. He put a burger, kiwi flavored drink and two chocolate puddings on his tray. All of the seats in the cafeteria were taken, though. "I wish for everyone to unfreeze." Everyone did just that. It was all normal again. They were completely oblivious to what happened. But Austin knew.

* * *

"Make sure this bathroom is cleaned thoroughly," Mrs. Shep said.

"Ok." Austin agreed. She walked out. He was given extra chores as part of his punishment. He knew it was going to take hours to clean the bathroom to his mother's standards. Then, he remembered the wishing stick. Austin walked down the hall to my bedroom to get it. He grabbed the wand off his bed. As he was about to leave, he saw Paula blocking the doorway.

"I'm telling Mom you're not cleaning," she said and cackled. "Mooooooooooooooom!"

"No, stop! I wish you would just freeze," Austin said. The ball began to glow, and Paula just stood there. She didn't move or talk. *Perfect, Paula can't annoy me.* Austin went into the bathroom. "I wish for the bathroom to be spotless," he said. Not even a second later, the bathroom was clean. The bathroom had a fragrant smell to it. The sink, toilet, and bathtub were cleaned perfectly. Austin went back to his room to undo the spell Paula was under.. She still stood in the doorway of his room. "I wish for Paula to unfreeze," Austin said. The ball glowed, and she unfroze.

"I'm telling Mom that you're not cleaning," she repeated.

"I already cleaned, bozo." Paula had a look of astonishment and then left the room. *She didn't suspect a thing. Wow. Oh wow. I can control everything!* Austin thought. The next day in gym class, Austin decided to take my fun with the wishing stick up a notch. He was in the locker room, getting changed. Steve Barrels came up to his locker.

"Austin's a wizard," he bellowed, pointing at him. The other boys started laughing at him. "He made Johnathan three feet tall. Now he doesn't want to go to school anymore." The boys' laughter continued to echo throughout the locker room. But Austin stood there, red-faced and angry. Steve grabbed the wishing stick from Austin's locker. "He used *this* to cast a spell on Johnathan."

"HEY, GIVE IT!"

"Catch it, Willy." Steve threw it at a red-haired boy in the back of the locker room. Willy caught it and gave it to a blond-haired boy next to him. "Don't let Austin get it," he instructed. *I have to get that stick back. I can't let those savages have it. I need to do something. Something that would put them in their place. I know just the thing.* Austin yelled, "I WISH FOR YOU ALL TO TURN INTO FLIES! "The stick glowed in the blond-haired boy's hand, and everybody turned into a fly. Plop! The wishing stick dropped to the floor. BUZZZZZZZ BUZZZZZ. They flew all around the locker room.

Quickly, Austin grabbed the wishing stick. A fly flew on his arm, but he swatted it away. *Perfect! Magnificent! It served them right for messing with me. With the wishing stick, no one is going to mess with me anymore.* Austin cackled at the top of my lungs.

"What's taking you boys so long?" Coach Andrews called from upstairs. Austin heard him walking to the locker room. He opened the door and went down the stairs. "Austin, where are the rest of the boys?" he asked, narrowing his eyes. Sweat poured down his face. A swarm of flies flew around him. "Gah! Where did all these flies come from?" Frantically, he swatted them away. "Well, speak up, Austin. Where'd the boys go?"

"I turned them into flies," Austin said.

"Don't play with me. Where are they?"

"I wish that you were a fly."

The wishing stick glowed, and Coach Andrews turned into a fly. He flew on my arm. Austin flicked him off. *Watch out, world, nothing's going to stop me.* Austin left the locker room and came into the hallway. The bell rang, and kids came rushing out of classrooms.

"Oh, hey, look, it's the wizard!" Suzie Barns said and pointed.

All of the kids in the hallway stopped and stared at Austin. There was silence.

"He's got his magic stick!" another kid said.

Suzie Barns stepped up to me. She grabbed me by the shoulders and shoved me against a locker.

"It's all your fault. You scared Johnathan away from this school. You have some nerve being here. Who do you think you are?"

Stop it. Stop it. Please stop.

"Gonna say nothing, huh? Let's see if you stay silent once I destroy you."

Stop. Don't make me do it. Don't make me do it. Please, God, don't make me do it.

Everything happened so fast. Suzie took a fist and punched Austin in the nose. His nose began to tingle, and something oozed out of it. He touched it. It was blood. Suzie grabbed Austin and tossed him on the floor. He hit the back of his head on the concrete floor. At that moment, He saw his life flash before my eyes. Paula's worm prank and Johnathan taking my comic book. He remembered the incident during gym last year.

Austin was in the shower, and Johnathan walked in on me and took pictures of my naked body. He was still able to hear all of their laughs. All the laughing that the boys did when they saw him butt naked. He could hear all the laughter at this point. Paula's high-pitched laugh, Jonathan's throaty laugh. Everybody who wronged him in his life. Everybody who broke him. *You guys made me do it. You broke me. Now it's time for my revenge.* Austin regained my vision. Everything came back to him.

"AHHHHHHHHHHHHHHHHHHHHHHHHHHHHH HHHHHHHHHH!" Austin screamed. "I WISH EVERYONE IN THIS FUCKING SCHOOL TO JUST DIEEEEEEEEE!"

The stick glowed. A wave of blue light sailed through the entire hallway. Everyone dropped to the floor, including Suzie. There was silence now. Everyone laid on the floor, with frozen petrified looks. *Yes, this feels good. This is the most powerful I've been in my fifteen years of life.*

Slowly, Austin walked through the hallway, laughing. He went downstairs to the front hall. In the middle of the front entrance were many dead bodies of boys and girls. Their eyes were closed and still had that petrified look. Austin passed the front office. Through the window, he saw the secretary with her face pressed down on the desk. He got to the front door and opened it. Austin turned and took one last look at the dead bodies.

"You all could burn in hell!" he yelled. Austin walked out of the door and left the school. He began to chuckle again. His laughter was uncontrollable. This feels great. *I'm so powerful! I have so much power in my hands! No one can take it away from me. No one. For once, I'm not this little punching bag. I am a warrior. A ruler. A lord. Everybody's gonna suffer. Everybody's going to die. This is going to be my world from now on. Everyone's going to feel my wrath. First order of business, Mom and Dad.*

Quickly, Austin ran toward home. In two minutes, he was there. Austin slammed the front door open. Mom and Dad came racing into the front hall.

"Austin, what are you doing home so early?" Mrs. Shep asked.

"Explain yourself, mister," Mr. Shep said.

"I don't need to answer to you guys anymore."

"Excuse me, what you say, boy?" Mrs. Shep asked.

"You heard me."

Austin paced back and forth. "No one can hurt me. I'm a ruler!"

"Boy, what are you talking about? What's in your hand?" Mrs. Shep asked. She pointed to the wishing stick.

Austin held it up and said, "This is my weapon. My weapon for greatness. I've got something better than Paula. I know Paula's the favorite. You let her get away with everything. Even practical jokes. She's hurt me. But you guys hurt me worst of all."

"Austin, stop playing with--,"

He cut his father off, "SHUT UP! You don't get to talk to me anymore. You clearly don't love me. You love Paula. You love this house. You love this neighborhood. You love this city. YOU LOVE EVERYTHING BUT ME! But guess what, I'm gonna destroy everything you love. I'm gonna make it rain. How about a nice meteor shower?

"What?"

"I WISH FOR A RAGING METEOR SHOWER."

They waited. At that moment, a meteor crashed through the house, and it exploded. Austin's burnt body came flying out of the explosion. The body face-planted onto the grass. Austin laid there, not moving. Next to him sat the wishing stick, broken into several pieces. The meteor shower continued to rage, blowing up more houses.

BACK TO 1942

I dashed downstairs to the kitchen for breakfast. I overslept. About to be late for school. Once I entered the kitchen, the smell of pancakes and garbage filled the air. The garbage bags were in front of the back door in the back of the kitchen. The trash hadn't been taken out. Mom and Dad were running around the kitchen with worried expressions. My little brother, Theo, sat at the table, already eating his breakfast.

"Why didn't you guys wake me up?" I asked.

Mom looked at me and said, "Sorry, sweetie. We forgot!"

"Hurry up and eat, Maya. We gotta go in five minutes," Dad said.

I went over by the stove and saw no more pancakes and sausage.

"Where's the food?" I demanded.

"There was a little bit left, so we gave it to Sam. He woke up first." Mom explained. From the table, Theo stuck his tongue out at me and laughed.

"Hahaha, you suck, Maya," he said.

. I grabbed the box of Fruity Pebbles off the top of the refrigerator and opened it. No cereal; It was all gone. "UGH! I HATE THIS!" I shouted and threw the empty box across the kitchen. *I'm just going to starve myself until lunchtime.* I walked out the front door, opened up Dad's SUV, and jumped in the backseat. Minutes later, the rest of my family came. Quickly, Dad drove us to school.

We pulled up in front of my school first, Hawthorne High. Theo smashed his Capri Sun, and the juice hosed out of the straw when I was about to get out. The juice splashed all over the front of my crisp white T-shirt.

"NOOO!" I yelled. "Why did you do that?"

Theo just laughed and laughed.

"You're just gonna have to suck it up, Maya," Mom said from the passenger seat.

"Yeah, Maya," Theo said and snickered.

"UGHHH, I HATE THIS FAMILY!" I yelled. I slammed the SUV door and stomped inside the school. I wrapped my arms around me to cover up the juice stain. I hated my family. I hated this so much. This kind of shit happened on the regular in the Kennedy family. It was like we were cursed. I loathed it so much.

* * *

The school was terrible. Kids had laughed at me about my stained shirt. All thanks to Theo. I hated that kid with a burning passion. I just wanted to punch his lights out. Him and the rest of my family.

Once I got home, Immediately, I ran into the kitchen for my leftovers. Last night, we ate shrimp scampi for dinner. It was so good that I made a plate of leftovers. I opened up the refrigerator and searched for the plate. It was not there. Gone.

Where are my leftovers? I wondered.

That was when Dad came into the kitchen, holding my plate of shrimp scampi!

"D-dad,"

"What?" he asked.

"T-those w-were my leftovers."

"Oh. I'm sorry. I didn't know."

My face turned hot red. Sweat rolled down my face.

"I HATE YOU!" I yelled. I stomped out the back door into the backyard. My kickball sat in the middle of the backyard. With all my strength, I gave it a hard kick. I always did this whenever I got mad. I would just kick it as many times as I could across the backyard until I felt better.

The ball sailed across the backyard and hit the back fence. I ran to go get it. As I ran, I hit a hard object on the ground. "Ow," I groaned. My toes hit the thing. I sat up and saw part of a shoebox poking out of the dirt. I grabbed it from under the dirt and examined the faded black box.

Is this a time capsule? How come no one in my family has seen it sticking out of the dirt. I opened the box and saw a red button labeled 1942. My gut feeling told me not to press the button. *What weirdo buries a shoebox with a button inside? Is there something wrong with it?* I wanted to press it anyway. Maybe it was one of those buttons that played a fun sound when pushed. I pushed the button hard and waited. No sound played, just silence.

Suddenly, everything around me began to spin. I felt confused, hazy, and woozy. I tried to scream, but no sound came out. Slowly, I began to fall, and everything faded to black. When my eyes began to adjust, I saw shops and people walking. I was in a town. My vision became clear. The town looked different. I saw a flower shop, a candy store, a small hardware store, and a general store. I've never seen those shops in the central part of my town before.

That wasn't the only weird part. People were walking through the town. I saw young ladies wearing a-line-skirts that went down to the knee. The women wore fedoras. *Why are they dressed like that?* I wondered. They were dressed like they came out of an old movie. Then, two men walked by, wearing blue sport coats with white pants; another man wore a gray trench coat.

What's going on? No one dresses like this anymore. It must be 1942. I did push the button. Definitely, I'm not at home. I've been sent back to 1942. That button must've sent me here.

"Hey, Maya, we thought we lost you," A woman's voice said behind me. I spun around and saw a man and a woman pushing a stroller.

"Who are you?"

"Behave yourself, Maya. You know we are your parents." The woman replied. *Huh? These people were saying they were my parents? Were they crazy?*

"Where's Theo?" I asked. The couple looked at each other, confused. "My brother?"

"You don't have a brother. You've always said boys were yucky."

"No, I have a brother! His name's Theo!" I yelled. The man and woman exchanged bewildered glances.

"She needs a nap," the man mouthed to the woman.

"I don't need a nap. I want to get out of 1942!"

"Come on, let's go," The woman said as she grabbed my hand. She held on tightly.

"Let go of me!" The woman ignored me. She tightened her grip, I couldn't let go.

"You're not my parents, and that baby is not my brother."

"Stop talking crazy, Maya. We are your parents, and that is your brother, Pat. End of discussion." the man snapped.

This has to be my family in this new reality. They could be much better than my original family. Maybe I'll just shut up and stay in 1942. It's better than staying back home with my terrible family.

"You shouldn't have run off like that. You know there are serial killers on the loose," the woman said. We continued to walk out of the town and toward the neighborhoods. We passed my neighborhood, Burbank, and walked into Nantucket.

"Umm, this neighborhood is wrong. Ours is back that way." I said, pointing backward.

"Nonsense, Maya. When we get home, you're going to rest. After you rest, we're gonna cook a nice feast."

We walked up to a one-story strawberry box house with white shutters. Once inside, I gasped. It was so old-fashioned. In the living room sat big pink couches along with shaggy pink carpeting. In the center of the room, instead of a TV, was a largely filled bookshelf. In the kitchen was a white retro-style refrigerator. Also, there was so much yellow in the room! The walls, the kitchen cabinets, and counters were yellow. There were frilly white curtains over the kitchen windows.

Houses aren't designed like this anymore. This is so old-school. What the fuck is this?

Where is my room? I went into a room at the end of the hall. Inside, it was a bedroom that had fake flower wallpaper. The same flower design was on my bedsheets and pillowcases. Pale sunlight came in through the frilly curtains. This room was hideous. I laid down on the bed. My new parents came into the room.

"Go to sleep Maya," New Mom whispered, caressing my long black hair. "Dinner will be ready once you wake up."

"Sleep tight," New Dad said.

Both of them left the room. They were lovely. They helped me go to sleep. My old parents never wished me Good night. They would just go right to bed. My eyelids began to feel heavier and heavier. I shut them and went fast asleep.

* * *

"Dinner time, honey," my new mom said. I opened my eyes and stared sleepily at her. My new mom grabbed me by the hand and led me out the room. Immediately, I whiffed the smell of lobster.

"You're gonna love this feast. I've cooked my finest dishes," she said.

We came into the kitchen. I gasped at what I saw at the table. There was a Jello Salad, plum charlotte and hot dog salad. The food looked so amazing. But the best dish was in the center of the table. The deviled lobster. I sat down and spooned some Jello salad on my plate.

"I don't know where your father went. He just snuck out of the house," My new mom said, "It's very unlike him to just leave."

"Weird," I said as I placed some of the hot dog salad on my plate. I grabbed a forkful of it, popped it in my mouth, and chewed. It wasn't so bad. It was a good combination of rubbery meat from the hotdog and crunch from the lettuce.

"I like this hotdog salad," I said.

"Thank you, dear," my new mom said.

At that moment, we heard the front door open and footsteps stomping through the front hall. The pungent odor of blood filled my nose. I covered my nose, and so did my new mom. Then, at the doorway stood my new dad. Sweat poured down his face, and he breathed heavily as if he had just run a marathon.

"I w-went for a run...t-trying to clear my mind," he said. "I'm gonna go shower."

He disappeared from the doorway and went on to the bathroom. The blood smell disappeared.

"Why did he smell like that?" I asked.

"I don't know," my new mom said.

We sat for a while, not eating.

"I've lost my appetite," I said.

My new mom nodded, and we both left the kitchen.

"I'm gonna go talk to your father once he finishes showering," my new mom said. She walked to the bedroom they shared. I followed her and went to mine. My new parents' bedroom was across the hall from mine. Both of us went inside our rooms.

* * *

On Saturday morning, I woke up for breakfast. I came into the kitchen and whiffed the smell of bacon. My new mom stood over the stove with her back to me. My new dad sat at the table, reading the newspaper.

"Good morning, Dad!" I chirped. I gave him a hug. But he didn't seem all too interested. He gave me a sour expression. I unwrapped the hug and sat back down at the table. My new mom staggered to the table with a pan of scrambled eggs. Something was off. For one, her eyes had heavy bags under them as if she hadn't slept. Her black hair was disheveled too.

She dumped all of the scrambled eggs onto my new dad's plate.

"Wait, Mom, what about me?"

"Hmm."

My new mom stared at me, "What do you mean?"

"Where's my eggs?" I asked.

My new mom ignored my question and brought pans of bacon and potatoes to the table. She loaded all of them on my new dad's plate.

"Wait, so I don't get breakfast,"

My new mom nodded.

"Why not?"

She just shrugged. My new dad smiled at me.

I got up from the table and stomped out of the room. I went up to my bedroom and slammed the door. *What's going on? Why aren't they feeding me? I* wondered. *Why are they acting so weird? It's like they don't even care.*

I laid on my bed and stared up at the ceiling. *Maybe I'm just overthinking it. Perhaps she cooked the last of the eggs, bacon, and potatoes. But still, why didn't she find something else for me to eat?* At least, back in the present, my family always had *something* for Theo and I to eat. I sighed. *Maybe I'll get dressed. There has to be something we can do in 1942. Something decent, right?*

I went into the closet and opened it. Inside were a-line dresses all in different colors. *Wow, these are so old-school. Yuck, I'm not wearing this.* I had no other choice, though. I pulled a red a-line dress off the hanger. Once I got dressed, I went to the living room, where my new parents sat on the couch, reading books.

"Can we please do something today?" I asked as I sat in the middle of them.

My parents looked at each other. My new dad gave my mother a disapproving look, and my mother nodded.

"No," my new mom said coldly.

"Why not?"

"Because I said so."

"B-b-but."

My new mom went back to reading her book. My face turned hot red. I clenched my fists. I stood up.

"BOTH OF YOU ARE NO FUN!" I thundered.

My new dad sat straight up. He pressed up against my face. His face was ketchup red.

"Go to your room. Don't come out for the rest of the day."

"Fine!"

I pounded up to my bedroom and started crying. *What was going on? Why don't they care about me? Why didn't they want to do anything?* Something was going on. The first day I was here, my new mom cooked a whole feast. My new parents actually spoke to me and treated me like I was their real child.

But ever since, that smell. That blood smell. My new dad was smelling like blood. Then, my new mom went to talk to him. This morning, she hadn't been the same since. *What happened to her? What did he say to her? Or worse, what did he do to her?* I wiped tears from my eyes. My eyelids felt heavy, and I dozed off to sleep.

* * *

I woke up drenched in sweat. I stared at the clock on my nightstand. It was 1:00A.M. *Oh, damn, did I really sleep through the whole day?* I turned on my bedside table lamp and saw I was still in my red a-line dress. As I was about to get out of bed, I heard the front door slam open.

Oh no, is it an intruder? I thought. With a swift motion, I turned my bedside table lamp off and hid under the covers. Stomping footsteps came closer and closer to my door. Suddenly, I caught a whiff of that smell. That horrible smell. That blood smell. *It has to be my new dad.*

The stomping footsteps stopped in front of my room. I laid in bed and gasped at what I saw through the crack of the door. I saw a shadow of a person peeking inside the room. I covered my mouth, trying not to speak or utter anything. Slowly, the person opened my door. They opened it up all the way.

The person crept closer to my bed. Moonlight reflected off of the person's face. It was my new dad! The smell of blood was even stronger than before. My new dad stood about two feet from my bed. He just stood there, watching me, not saying anything. Finally, after minutes of utter silence, he whispered in the coldest and unkind voice, "I've got plans for you tomorrow, kid."

Then, he turned around and walked out of the room. He shut the door behind him. I sat up. My heart was racing. Sweat was running down my face like a waterfall. *What the fuck is going on here? Why is my new dad acting so creepy? What did he mean by plans? What's he going to do to me?*

I breathed heavily. Maybe he was going to do the same thing he did to my new mom. He was probably going to do something horrible to me. Just thinking about this made me tear up. I needed to get out of 1942 and away from this family. I missed my old reality. I missed the crazy mornings. I missed Theo, even though he drove me crazy. I still loved him.

I wanted to go back home. Back to my real family. How was I supposed to do that? I didn't know. Was I actually stuck here forever? Do my real parents know that I left? Are they searching for me? Even if I did come back to the present, I wouldn't tell them where I went. They wouldn't believe me and think that I ran away on purpose. That was when it hit me. My old house. My old neighborhood. I had found the 1942 button in the backyard in the present. The creator of the time button must be living in my old home right now! I needed to go there in the early morning. *Yes, this is a good idea.*

Second thoughts came into my mind. *What if the creator is not there. What if this could be the new normal for me.* Whatever was about to happen to me tomorrow was going to be the end of me. I couldn't let that happen. I just couldn't.

* * *

The next morning, I got out of bed to go downstairs. My legs were shaking. I didn't know what this man was going to do to me. I opened my bedroom door, but it was locked. I wiggled and jiggled on the doorknob. Locked. Locked from the outside.

Did these people lock me in here? I wondered. *What's going on?* Damnit, how was I supposed to sneak out? I paced back and forth around the room. *Was this the plan that the man had? What's he gonna do now?*

At that moment, I heard the sound of keys clattering. I stared at the door. The doorknob clicked and began to turn. The door opened, and there stood my new Mom and Dad. They had glares on their faces. My new dad had blood smeared on his cheeks. He carried something behind his back. I tried not to say anything, but it all just came out.

"What the hell is going on? Why was Dad in my room last night? What are your plans? Why am I not getting fed? W-what,"

"It's about time, you know the truth," my new dad said softly.

"What's the truth? Tell me!"

My new mom stepped closer to me and said, "Maya, your father is a--"

"Serial killer," my new dad finished.

I gulped. *Serial killer? So that must explain the blood.*

"I talked to your father the other day about the blood smell. I always suspected that he was a serial killer. Once, I told him that. He threatened to kill me. I begged and pleaded, hoping he would give in. He gave me an ultimatum."

My new mom coughed and continued, "I had to serve him all of his favorite foods and do everything he says, or else he was going to kill me. I had to give in. My life was on the line, and I loved him s-s-so much!"

Tears formed in the corners of her eyes. "I'm sorry, Maya."

"I'm the killer of children. I've killed over ten kids. I've always hated them. Those chubby piles of mucus. They're a disgrace to this world. I've been ridiculed by them my whole fucking life!"

My new dad stepped up to me and wrapped his left arm around my neck. He pulled the object out from behind his back. It was a shiny butcher knife. He gently caressed the blade against my face.

"Ever since you were born. I couldn't stand the sight of you. Now it's time to go!"

"No!" I yelled.

"Honey, please don't," my new mom said.

"How about a nice stab in the eye? Does that sound good to you?"

"Let me go!"

My new dad ignored me and raised the knife. With quick thinking, I stomped my foot hard on my dad's foot.

"Owww!" my new dad yelped. He took his hands off of my neck and started rubbing his left foot. That was my cue to leave. I ran out of the room.

"COME BACK HERE!" my new dad shouted from behind me.

"Don't let him get you!" my new mom shouted.

I ran through the house and reached the front door. Quickly, I opened it and ran outside. My new dad's stomping footsteps were quickly gaining on me. I ran down the street, still running, not stopping for anything. I looked back and saw my new dad catching up to me. His stare was more menacing than ever. His brown eyes were trained onto me. *Oh no, he's gonna catch up. I need to move faster!*

We ran all the way through Burbank until we got to the end. I saw the Nantucket neighborhood sign. I ran into it, and my new dad followed. Quickly, I scanned the houses, looking for my old house. Finally, I saw my red brick two-story home. I galloped up to the front door and banged on it hard. "OPEN UP! OPEN UP! OPEN THE DOOR! I NEED HELP! HELP ME PLEASE!" I screamed at the top of my lungs.

I saw my new dad run up the front porch. At that moment, a middle-aged man answered the door. He saw my new dad and shoved me inside. Quickly, he shut the door and locked it. It was too late for my new dad. He started banging on the door with all of his strength. "I WANT THE GIRL! I WANT THE GIRL!" he was yelling.

He shouted for a few more minutes. He gave up and left after that.

"Thank you so much!" I said. "That was my crazy father in this new reality in 1942! Are you the creator of the button? Can you send me back? Please!"

The man nodded. "I see. You found my time button for 1942."

"Yes, do you have a button that takes me to the present? You have to! You must! I wanna go back to my real family!

Th-those people were horrible! They almost killed me! I have nowhere else to go but home! Please help me!"

The man stared at me for a while.

"Come with me," he finally said. He led me upstairs to a room at the end of the hall.   Inside, looked like a laboratory. The room had green lighting and was extremely messy. There was a large table in the back of the room that had all sorts of weird gadgets and experiments. Boxes were stacked in all corners of the room. His bed was unmade and had strange green stains on the sheets.

The man said, "My name is Dr. James. I create time machines to send me back to different periods." I listened attentively.

"I created the 1942 time machine because that was the year when I did my best experiments. I would be eighty in the present day, but I was twenty in 1942. Time travel seemed to have kept me alive. Because you live at my old house in the present, that means the other version of me would've been dead."

"Morbid," I said. "What do you mean by the other version? He didn't answer my question. He went on saying, "I had buried the 1942 Button hoping no one would ever find it and keep it as something for myself."

"Well, I found it. Do you have a button to take me back to the present?"

Dr. James took a long pause. "Yes, I do," He went underneath the table and pulled out a brown box. He rummaged through and pulled out a green button. I made a grab for it, but he moved it away.

"There are some things you need to know first." Dr. James said.

"What?" I asked.

"First, once you get back to the present. You have to find the "other" you back at your house. There are two of you. One in 1942 and the other in the present. Second, Once you find the other "you" you have to lure her into the backyard and open up the time portal to send her back. She's gonna die because you weren't alive in 1942."

"How do I open up the time portal?"

"By this chant, "Once in the past, now in the present, go back to 1942 for good." Understand?"

I nodded. This was a mouthful for me.

"Now press the button to go back to the present." Dr. James said.

"Wait, you not gonna come back to the present as well," I asked.

"Are you kidding? I like it here. This truly feels like my home. Go ahead. You go back to the present, do you hear me, girl?"

I nodded again. "Alright." I was going to do it. Whatever it took, to go back home to my real family. That was where I belonged. I stepped forward and pushed the green button hard. Everything went purple, and the room began to fade… fade… and fade until everything came back into view. Dazed, I stared around. I recognized a house, my white painted house!. I stood across from it, staring up at it. That's when I saw my mother come out of the house. My real mother! I even saw my bratty younger brother Theo behind her, holding a trash bag. I actually missed him!

"Now, you take out the trash, mister. I don't want to hear any more excuses." Mom told Theo curtly.

"Yes, mam." He began to move toward me.

"Theo!" I yelled. I ran across the street, holding out my arms, ready to hug him. "I've missed you. I ran in front of Theo, blocking his path. To my horror, he walked right through me and continued walking.

What… what just happened? Why… Why did he go through me? Am I a ghost? I thought. Suddenly, it hit me. He couldn't see me because I was not the real Maya to him. He thought the other Maya was the only Maya. I didn't exist to him.

"Nononono," I said aloud. "I've got to lure that stupid fake Maya outside to the backyard. I'm the real Maya." Quickly, I ran inside the house and ran through the living room. I found my real dad sitting on the couch watching TV.

"Hi, Dad!" I said. He didn't respond. He couldn't see me either. I advanced forward and ran upstairs to my room. I flung open the door to find the "Other Maya" sitting on the foot of my bed.

She turned around and stared at me.

"GO BACK TO 1942, YOU FAKE!" I yelled.

"Oh, silly Maya. There's nothing you can do. I'm going to take over your life forever and replace you as the original Maya!" She said calmly.

"Oh, there's something I can do!" I ran up to her and pushed her off the bed. She fell hard to the floor.

"YOU WEAK LITTLE GIRL, YOU CAN'T STOP ME!" The Other Maya said.

I punched her in the face repeatedly, pinning her down to the ground. The Other Maya stood up and pushed me down. I got back up and gave her the hardest push. The Other Maya stumbled back across the room and fell out the large open window.

"AHHHHHHHHHHHHHHHHHHHHHHHHHHHH!" She fell down two stories and hit the ground hard. I watched her lay on the grass. She didn't make any move. Not even a sound from her.'

Is she dead? Did I kill her? I wondered. Quickly, I ran out of the room and went outside to the backyard. The Other Maya still laid there, not moving. I walked over to her and examined her.

"GOTCHA!" The Other Maya screamed. She grabbed my foot and knocked me down on the grass. She sat on top of my back. I thrashed and kicked, trying to break free. She was so strong. I heard one of my bones CRACK. "Give up, Maya. You lost, and I won. Looks like you're going back to 1942." The Other Maya said. *No, no, no! I can't let her win!* With all of my might, I pushed myself upright and ran across the backyard. "Hey, you get back here!" The Other Maya shouted. She was chasing after me. But I was ready to do what I had to do.

"Once in the past, now in the present. Go back to 1942 for good!" I yelled. That's when the ground began to shake. Then, a large gaping hole with purple smoke began to form. The Other Maya started pushing me again, pushing me towards the portal. I stood inches from it.

"Bye-bye, Maya." The Other Maya said. She gave me one final push, but I caught my strength and didn't fall in. I turned around and pushed the Other Maya into the portal. "NOOOOOOOOOOOOOOOOOOOOOOOOOOOOOOO!" The Other Maya moaned. She slid into the void. Her hands were up in the air and defeat. Tears rolled down her face.

"I WILL GET YOU FOR THIS SOMEDAAAAAAAY! I'LL BE BACKKKKKKKKKKKKKKK!" She slid down faster into the void and disappeared into the ground. I could still hear her screams from inside the portal. They began to fade quickly. The portal closed back up and became a patch of grass again. It was like it never appeared.

Sorry Other Maya. I'm the real Maya of the Kennedy Family. I will and always will be. No one can replace my real family. At that moment, Sam came bursting outside into the backyard, holding a football.

"Maya, what are you doing?" He asked. He could see me! Yes! It really did work! I gave him a big hug.

"I've missed you!" I gushed.

"What are you talking about? You were always here, weirdo." He unwrapped the hug. "Wanna play football?" Sam asked.

"Sure."

We sprinted across the backyard. As we ran, Sam tripped and fell to the ground. He got back up and ran inside the house.

"Mom, Maya pushed me!" he shouted.

What a brat! But I still loved him.

DON'T BREAK
THE ICE...

Old Mrs. Jensen was gone. She left us. Well, not like that. She had left for another art conference. I was excited that Mrs. Jensen was gone because my friend, Julie, and I got to play or snoop around on her lawn. Every time she went on a trip, we snuck into her yard and goofed around. We did this because she had the most enormous yard in the neighborhood. Plus, there was absolutely nothing to do in Penngrove.

"Julie, Jensen's gone," I said over the phone.

"She is?"

"Yes, let's go outside and play."

"Okay, okay, I'll meet you there."

She hung up, and I put on my boots, coat, and gloves. I walked downstairs and out the front door. Of course, the cold made my nose run. Snow was falling heavily. There was already about four feet of snow on the ground. Perfect. Just enough for a snowball fight. Across the street, I saw Julie standing next to Ms. Jensen's ice sculpture. As an artist who carved ice sculptures, Mrs. Jensen loved the winter. It was a six-foot-tall gleaming ice sculpture of herself. It had her straight hair, her soulless eyes, and her toothy grin carved into it. The body of the sculpture was curvy in the right spots and showed Ms. Jensen's large boobs carved into it. I walked over to Julie, and we did our signature handshake.

"Let's start playing Freeze Tag," Julie said as she wiped the snow off of her black front ponytail. She had a face full of makeup even though we were just going to play outside. Not to mention, the makeup always looked horrible. She wore so much pink blush and pink eyeshadow. It made her look like a rabbit. I never told her that it looked bad, but all the kids at school thought it did. I figured Julie would stop doing makeup after the teasing. But she didn't.

"We need more people," I said. That's when I saw Kyle and Kris walking down the sidewalk. They were fourteen-year-old twin brothers. Kyle had lime green hair. Most of the dye was coming off to reveal his natural black hair color. Kris had his wild black hair. Kyle dyed his hair to let people know that he was different from his brother.

"There's Kyle and Kris," I said, pointing. Quickly, I grabbed Julie and dragged her behind the front bush. They hadn't seen us yet.

"Hey!" Julie exclaimed.

"Shush, Kyle, and Kris will hear us," I whispered, "Let's throw snowballs at them." Julie and I made snowballs and then pelted them at Kyle and Kris.

"Hey,." Kyle complained. Snow had gotten all over his hair. He patted the snow from his coat as he bent down to grab his snow ammo. I just did my hair." Kris made a snowball and threw it at my face.

"Oh, you're gonna get it now!" I yelled. We fought and laughed until finally falling down to make snow angels.

"Let's play Freeze Tag," Julie suggested.

Kris and Kyle nodded, and we all started to play our first round of tag. Julie was "it," and we all ran from her. I got tagged by her. Kyle unfroze me, and we continued playing. We started the second round, and I was "it" this time.

"Aaaaaand start!" Julie declared. The game began, and I started to go after Kris since he ran the slowest. I sprinted after him, so deep in concentration that I didn't see the ice sculpture. I ran smack into the sculpture. It shook and fell to the ground hard. The sculpture shattered into a million pieces on top of the snow.

"Oh no!" I shrieked. Everyone paused and stared at the mess I had created.

"You're so dead," Kyle said.

"What are we going to do about this? Maybe we can tell—" everybody started to leave.

"Hey, come back," I ordered. Julie, Kyle, and Kris were running away. Some friends they were. I decided to race home out of fear. I ran inside and went upstairs. What was I going to tell Mrs. Jensen? She would kill us if she found out that we were on her lawn. She always got mad if a kid broke something around her house.

Last summer, a boy named Tom was playing on her lawn and accidentally broke her lawn gnomes. Ms. Jensen came home and caught him. She yelled at him for hours and persuaded him to go inside. Tom never went out of the house, and it was rumored that Ms. Jensen killed Tom because of the broken lawn gnomes. There was another rumor that he was just locked away in her house.

That night, I was in bed, trying to shake the ice sculpture guilt off. I felt cold underneath the covers. I looked at my window to the right of my bed. It was shut tight. The breeze wasn't coming in through there. It was so cold in the room, I sneezed. *Why's it so cold in here?* Mom and Dad never turned the AC on in the winter. That's when I saw a large looming shadow across the room. It looked like a person. Who's that?

I turned on my bedside table lamp and looked across the room.

"Oh nooo! It can't be!" I saw Ms. Jensen's ice sculpture. Its soulless eyes weren't soulless. They were bright yellow and lit up the whole room. Its grin was now a sadistic smirk. The sculpture moved closer to my bed. It leaned forward until we were face to face.

"Why did you break me?" The raspy voice sounded just like Ms. Jensen's. "Why did you break me?" I laid there frozen, unable to speak. "WHY DID YOU BREAK ME!" It yelled.

"AHHHHHHHHHHH!"

Mom and Dad burst into the room. The ice sculpture vanished into thin air.

"Honey, what happened?" Mom asked.

"M-m-ms. Jensen's ice sculpture," I stammered.

"Just a bad dream," Dad said, "Now go back to sleep." Mom tucked me in under the covers, and they left the room. I stared up at the ceiling wide-eyed.

I knew I wasn't getting any sleep that night. I thought the ice sculpture broke. Why did it appear in my room? I broke the sculpture. Is it...alive?

The next morning, I walked with Julie to school. Julie was going on and on about a new TV show she started watching, but I was tired, dead tired. Something caught my eye across the street. On the lawn across the street, I saw the ice sculpture. It waved and smiled at me.

"Earth to Beth! Earth to Beth!" Julie yelled, waving her hands in front of me.

"Oh."

"Did you listen to anything I said?"

"I...uh...I...saw Ms. Jensen's ice sculpture in my room last night," I said. "And I saw it across the street just now."

"Give me a break," Julie said. She didn't believe me. We ignored it and kept walking to school. Maybe I was crazy.

In math class, I couldn't concentrate on the lesson. My teacher, Mrs. Bell, kept pointing to the board. The numbers looked like squiggles and gibberish. I didn't understand them.

I was so tired from the lack of sleep that I dozed off. I found myself in a field. It seemed to stretch for miles. I didn't know where it ended. I saw a single tree in the distance. It was an oak tree with a thick trunk. It was hot and sunny. Sweat poured down my face. Water, I needed a drink badly. I wiped beads of sweat from my forehead. Then, the sun went down, and it was cloudy. It became cold out. Without a coat, I shivered, smoke came out of my mouth, and my teeth chattered. I wiped off my nose snot with the back of my hand. When I looked up, there it was, the ice sculpture.

Quickly, it made its way toward me until we were face to face.

"What do you want?"

"You broke me. Now feel the cold." It said calmly.

It began to blow on me. The wind or its breath was strong. I flew backward.

"Stop!" I demanded.

"More cold. More cold." The ice sculpture chanted. It blew until I was frozen like a popsicle. I had become an ice sculpture. That's when I woke up.

"Beth Thompson, Beth Thompson, Sleeping in my class!" Mrs. Bell said. I was drooling. Everybody in the class started laughing and pointing at my drool. Even Julie, Kris, and Kyle.

'Stop.' 'Stop.' 'Don't kill me, Mrs. Jensen, '" Kris teased. Everyone laughed even harder.

"See me after class." Mrs. Bell said, with her arms crossed tightly. Everybody in the class continued to laugh. I could feel the redness on my face. "Settle down, everybody. Who can explain the conflict of Lucy Terry's poem, Bars Fight?" The bell rang, and I stayed after with Mrs. Bell. She gave me a stern lecture about getting enough sleep and paying attention. She didn't punish me, which was good. Later, Julie had to leave early for a dental appointment. I walked home alone after school. I saw the stupid ice sculpture pop up in front of me.

"Why do you keep terrorizing me?"

"You broke me, and now you must freeze." The ice sculpture shards began to blow when a voice behind me said: "Beth, who are you talking to?" I spun around and saw Kyle and Kris. The ice sculpture vanished.

"What's going on, Beth?" Kyle asked. "That incident in class was—"

"The ice sculpture keeps terrorizing me.," I interrupted.

"You see things.," Kris said.

"N-n-no way. It's alive." I ran from them. They didn't believe me. Who would believe me? I got to my house and stormed inside. Mom and Dad had said they were going to be working late, so they weren't home. I went upstairs to my room. Once I got inside, the ice sculpture was waiting for me.

"Get out of my house!"

"Enjoy the cold." The ice sculpture growled. Shards began to blow, and snowflakes started to fall in my room. Snow flew everywhere, and my room was getting colder and colder. I had to stop it. *Wait a minute, the heat melts ice, yeah. Great idea.* So I was going to turn the heat up on the entire house. I ran out of the room.

"Going somewhere, dearie?" The ice sculpture called after me. It chased after me, but I ran faster. I went downstairs into the front hallway.

I walked up to the thermostat. Usually, I wasn't allowed to touch it, but I had no choice. I moved the dial to the right on the thermostat.

70 degrees,

75 degrees,

80 degrees,

90, degrees

100, degrees,

120 degrees! I had the thermostat all the way up. It couldn't get any hotter. The whole room started to feel hot. Sweat poured down my face. The ice sculpture came in the front hallway. It wasn't melting, though.

"Hahahaha, nice try, dearie! You destroyed the one outside, not can't destroy me!" it cried. The ice sculpture started to blow cold wind despite being one-hundred and twenty degrees, I got cold. My teeth began to chatter while the rest of my body shivered. Something else. I had to think of something else. But I had to think fast before this sculpture turned me into a human popsicle. My hands and my face were becoming numb.

I had an idea. I shattered the ice sculptures into a million pieces when they fell for the first time. Maybe I could use something to break it into even smaller pieces. I ran into the kitchen and to the drawers. I had the perfect idea for a weapon. The ice sculpture followed me.

"You will become ice!" it declared. I rummaged through the drawers frantically. Then I found it, an ice pick. The ice sculpture came into the kitchen.

"Nowhere to run," it said menacingly, "I've got you allllll to myself now."

"Bye, bye," I said. I walked over to the sculpture and tried to jam the ice pick. But the ice sculpture blew on me.

Its breath knocked me backward, causing me to hit my head on the sink.

"Ow," I moaned. The ice pick flew out of my hands and to the other side of the kitchen.

Noooooo! The ice sculpture loomed above me. It had a menacing expression.

"DO YOU WANT COLD?" it yelled. That's when I crawled on the kitchen floor. I saw the ice pick under the kitchen table.

"Oh, no, you don't!" The ice sculpture chased me. I crawled faster and faster until I got under the kitchen table. I dove for the ice pick.

"BE ICE!" the ice sculpture yelled. He blew, causing snowflakes to fall in the kitchen.

I crawled in front of the sculpture and stabbed it in the legs. The legs began to crack.

"NooooOooooooo!" the ice sculpture bellowed. I stabbed it in the face. The cracks moved up and down the ice sculpture. Then, it shattered into a million pieces and fell to the ground.

I stared in amazement. The snow and the shattered ice disappeared into thin air. I was so proud I defeated the ice sculpture. There was still one problem, though: I had to face Mrs. Jensen.

* * *

Mrs. Jensen returned from her vacation. She went ballistic when she saw the ice sculpture was gone. I went over to her house and apologized. She accepted my apology very nicely.

After that, I celebrated with my friends with some pizza. A week after that, Mrs. Jensen put another ice sculpture in her front yard. It was a giant eight-foot swan. One day, Mrs. Jensen left her home, and I decided to play on her lawn. I was going to be careful this time. I invited Julie, Kris, and Kyle, and we walked over there. Once we got to the lawn, The swan seemed to lift its head and wink at us while it uttered, "Off Jensen's lawn or die…"

GRANNY'S LITTLE BABY

I sat in the car while Mom drove me to Grandma Esther's house. I haven't seen my Grandma since I was two.

"Why couldn't I stay home alone. I'm fourteen."

"Fourteen is too young," Mom said, "Once you turn sixteen, then maybe you can stay home alone."

"Ugh, you're so unfair!" I kicked my feet on the seat. The strap on my black dress shoes unbuckled. I hated those shoes along with the big white dress I wore. I looked like a doll. These were the only kinds of clothes I owned. Mom made me dress like this so I could look more feminine. But to me, it made me look babyish. Mom still treated me like I was two years old.

"I hope she doesn't do any of that weird sorcerer stuff around you." Mom said. "Hopefully, she keeps to her word." Grandma Esther used to be a sorcerer when she was younger. She liked to cast spells like turn people into toads and stuff like that. Mom was afraid of her casting some kind of spell on me. That's why I hadn't seen her in so long. Grandma had promised that she wouldn't cast any spells. Plus, all of our other relatives were busy or on vacation, so they couldn't watch me.

We finally pulled up to the driveway of Grandma Esther's house. Her house was big with black shutters and large windows. Grandma Esther stood out on the front porch. She waved at us when we pulled into the driveway. Grandma Esther was a small and frail lady. She had straight gray hair with white highlights. She wore a pink, flowered house dress and matching house shoes.

We got out of the car, and Mom took the bags from the trunk.

"Jackie, darling," Grandma Esther gushed. She came walking up to us with a baby bottle in her hand. She gave me a big hug and a wet kiss on the cheek.

"Yuck. I hate that," I said, rolling my eyes.

"Jackie!" Mom said, glaring at me.

Grandma Esther's smile faded. "Well, I haven't seen you in so long."

"I don't wanna be treated like a baby, thank you."

Both of them stared at me in bewilderment.

"I'm in a hurry. I'll see you in a couple of days," Mom said. She gave me a quick hug and left. It was just Grandma Esther and me. I could tell that Mom didn't want to be around her.

"Come inside dear, I have a treat for you." She plastered a warm smile on her face and grabbed me by the hand. She dragged me inside. I was greeted with a strong cinnamon aroma coming from the kitchen.

Grandma led me to the living room. There was a TV, a large velvet couch, and two lounge chairs. The weird part about the living room was the many baby pictures hanging on the wall. They were of different boys and girls. Grandma led me into the kitchen.

"Sit, sit," she insisted, pointing to a small table in the corner of the kitchen.

"Grandma, why do you have a ton of baby pictures hanging on the wall in the living room?"

She ignored me. I watched her stir something in a green bowl with the wooden spoon on the counter. Then, she brought it over to me.

"I made it myself." It was a bowl of applesauce.

I haven't eaten this since I was a baby. Why couldn't Grandma have just cooked regular food for me? "I don't want to eat this. I'm not a kid.".

"Eat up!" Grandma Esther insisted, pushing the bowl in front of me. I stared at the bowl. The applesauce looked so gross. It wasn't the normal light orange color applesauce. This one was a much darker brown color.

"You're not leaving until you eat," Grandma Esther said. Then, she burst out laughing.

Reluctantly, I picked up the spoon and scooped up some applesauce. I shoved it into my mouth. There was a lot of cinnamon in the applesauce! I choked it down anyway to satisfy Grandma Esther. It was so sweet. "Mmmm. Good."

"Eat the rest of it," Grandma Esther commanded. She had a look of excitement in her eyes. She wanted to watch me eat it. I finished the bowl. It actually tasted pretty good once I ate more.

She had a big hungry grin on her face and twitched her eyes.

"Good," I said.

"I'm glad you liked it," she said while grabbing my bowl.

"I'll show you to your room." Grandma Esther led me upstairs into a dark hallway. She led me into a room at the end of the hall. The room was painted pink with a single dresser, bedside table, closet, and bed.

"I'm glad you liked the applesauce," Grandma Esther said, "It'll be a side dish for dinner." She let out a chuckle and left the room. *Applesauce for dinner?* I thought.

* * *

For dinner, that night was chicken pot pie, roasted potatoes, and a huge bowl of applesauce. For desert, a large apple pie! As I ate, Grandma Esther kept looking at me with a creepy grin of satisfaction.

She's probably happy that someone is enjoying her food. I thought. I had gone with that theory. But when I woke up the next morning, I didn't think that was the case. When I opened my eyes, I felt...smaller.

I saw bars around me. Bars? I looked around. It was a crib. Then, I glanced up and saw toys hanging over me. I examined my hands. They were so small and stubby. Then, all of it hit me like a tidal wave. The bars, the toys, the hands. I was a baby!

I stared down at my clothes. I didn't have any clothes on, only a diaper.

"Goo goo gaa," I blurted out. Oh no! I was starting to talk like a baby. I moved around the crib, seeing if I was able to walk. I stood up and walked. I could walk perfectly.

Good, I was able to walk. I thought. My body had to be at least two years old. I laid down in the crib. How did this happen? Suddenly, Grandma Esther burst into the room, breaking through my thoughts.

"Hi, Jackie pie! Did you sleep well?" She asked in a sing-songy voice. She picked me up out of the crib and held me up. I could smell her hot breath on my face. "Time for some food," Grandma Esther said. She carried me out of the room and downstairs to the kitchen. She set me down on a high chair in the kitchen. Grandma Esther went into the cupboard and pulled out a can of creamed carrots.

Yuck. I hated carrots, even when I was a fourteen year old. She s made an airplane motion with a spoonful of carrots towards my mouth.

"Here comes the airplane," Grandma Esther said. She kept hovering the spoon in front of my mouth. As it got closer, I knocked the spoon out of her hand, and it fell to the floor. "Jackie, Bad girl!" Grandma Esther cleaned up the spilled carrots and rinsed off the spoon. She held out another spoonful of carrots for me. "Here comes the airplane," she repeated. This time I decided to just eat them. I ate the carrots from the spoon.

Yuck! They didn't taste good. But I forced myself to swallow them.

"Good job," Grandma Esther said, slapping me a high five. *You wouldn't let me leave unless I ate them.* I thought bitterly.

Later, Grandma changed my diaper and put me in a pink Care Bears shirt and jeans.

"I set up a playdate for you," Grandma Esther said. A playdate. Oh no. This couldn't possibly get any worse. Something weird was going on, and I was going to find out.

The doorbell rang, and she brought me downstairs in the living room. Grandma Esther answered the door. She brought in a younger lady I didn't recognize into the living room.

The young lady was chubby and had straight brown hair and blue eyes. Behind the lady, a baby boy was sucking his thumb. He was wearing a Smurfs T-shirt.

"This is Jackie," Grandma Esther said, introducing me.

"She looks mad," the lady commented. *You would be mad too if you transformed into a baby in one night.*

"This is Brian." Grandma Esther pointed to the baby boy. Brian sat in front of me and waved. His mother put a toy firetruck and Hot Wheels cars down in front of him.

I decided to play with them anyway. I made a grab for the firetruck, but Brian snatched it out of my hand.

"Mine," he whined.

"Brian, share with Jackie," his mother scolded. He put on a pouty face and gave me back the toy.

This was going to be some playdate. I thought.

The playdate ended later, and Brian and his mother left. Grandma Esther and Brian's mother kept watching us the whole time, making the playdate awkward. Brian wouldn't let me play with his toys, so he got sent home early as punishment.

For dinner, Grandma Esther just gave me a big tub of applesauce. She put me in the crib right after dinner. I couldn't sleep. I knew exactly who turned me into a baby. It was Grandma Esther.

That had to be it. The applesauce, her hungry expression when she watched me eat, the baby pictures. Grandma Esther turned me into a baby. But why? Why did she turn me into a baby?

I had to change myself back before Mom picked me up tomorrow. I had to figure out how she did this and why. I needed to undo it. Like my mom said, she was a sorcerer. I knew she was only just trying to do what was best for me. I wished I was fourteen again. I missed being able to put my own clothes on, eat whatever I wanted, and control my body. That was something I took for granted. For what seemed like forever, I managed to shut my eyes and fall asleep.

* * *

"Your mommy comes home today," Grandma Esther said, while she put my clothes on.

Great, but I'm still a baby.

"I'm going to convince your mom to let me keep you. You can be my child forever and ever and ever," she said. Grandma Esther gave me a big hug.

Oh no, Grandma. I'm not going to be stuck with a crazy old coot like you. She hugged me for the longest time and finally took me downstairs for breakfast. Grandma Esther gave me a spoonful of creamed peas this time. I ate them even though they were gross. I was pretty hungry. Grandma made me eat the whole jar of creamed peas.

At around one p.m, I was set down for an afternoon nap. Mom had said she was picking me up at three o'clock. I heard Grandma Esther taking soft steps back downstairs. This was my chance to find out how to change the spell.

I had to sneak into her room to see what she was hiding. I needed to get out of my crib first. I sat straight up in the crib. My mom always said I escaped the crib all the time when I was a baby.

I climbed up the bars and jumped out of the cage. I hit the floor hard, almost banging my knee. I stumbled on my feet and began to walk out of the room. Conveniently, Grandma Esther had left the door wide open. I walked out of the room and into the hallway. As I walked, I tripped over my foot, hitting the ground hard.

"Ow," I moaned. I listened for Grandma Esther. She didn't hear me it seemed. Good, that was a close one. I sat back up and continued walking. Grandma Esther's room was at the end of the hall.

I stumbled down the hallway, being cautious with each step. Finally, I made it to Grandma Esther's room. The door was ajar. I was greeted with the smell. It made my nostrils swell, and I sneezed. "How does Grandma stand it in here?" I said aloud. In the room, there was an unmade bed, a desk, a dresser. But on top of the desk was a stack of three leather-bound books. Grandma's spellbooks, I assumed. I walked over to the desk to check them out. I climbed up the chair and stood upright.

I read the tiny type on the books. The book on the top of the stack read: *Lizard to Human.* Another text read: *Newt to Frog.* When I was about to read the last book title. I saw a piece of aged parchment paper. What it said caught my eye. It said: How to turn a baby back into a kid. Use the Kid Morphing Drink.

Kid Morphing Drink? What is that? I wondered. I had to find it. Maybe Grandma Esther had hidden it in the room. I got off the chair and back down on the floor. I looked under the desk. Nothing there.

I looked under the bed. I couldn't see much of anything under there. It was total blackness. Then, I saw something that looked like a bottle about a few feet in front of me.

The outside light showed its silhouette on the carpet. I crawled under the bed to grab it. It was about the size of a wine bottle. I grabbed it and carefully crawled from under the bed.

I read the small type on the bottle: It read: Kid Morphing Drink. Yayyyyyy! I had found what I was looking for. There was instruction on the back of the bottle: ***Drink only one sip or else you'll age too fast.*** I hopped on the bed. The bottle was full.

I tried to squeeze open the bottle, but my hands were too tiny. I squeezed it with all my might and managed to pop it open. The liquid smelled like apple cider. I drank a sip of it. It definitely didn't taste like apple cider. It tasted bitter. I wanted to spit it out, but I managed to swallow it.

Suddenly, I began to change. I felt woozy. I started to grow bigger and bigger. Everything was getting smaller. Then the feeling stopped.

I checked myself out. I saw my hands. My hands! They were normal-sized. I got up to look in the mirror and saw my puny fourteen-year-old self! I could walk on two feet! I can speak!

"Yes. It worked," I said aloud. I shot my fists up in the air.

"What do you think you're doing?" I heard a voice cry. I spun around and saw Grandma Esther in the doorway. She had an angry expression on her face. In horror, I dropped the Kid Morphing Drink.

The glass shattered, and brown liquid oozed out onto the carpet.

"No more cure," Grandma Esther murmured.

"Why did you turn me into a baby?" I demanded.

She cleared her throat. "I get so lonely. I want a kid to hug and cuddle. Since your mom didn't want me to see you anymore. I thought I would turn you into a sweet and precious baby."

"What?" I shrieked. Grandma Esther walked closer to me. She stepped up to me until we were face to face.

"You need more applesauce….now." Suddenly, she let out a loud squeal of pain.

"YOOOOOOW!" I looked down and saw she stepped on the glass shards from the bottle. Grandma Esther held out a hand to grab me, but I ran away. I looked back and saw Grandma Esther limping behind me.

I sprinted downstairs and raced to the kitchen. I didn't know how to stop her. I had to think. Grandma Esther limped into the kitchen. I saw blood trickling out her foot.

"Baby Jackie! Baby Jackie! Oh, how I want Baby Jackie!" She said in a sing-songy voice. She limped up to me, holding out her hands.

Out of the corner of my eye, I saw a bowl of applesauce. That was it. If the applesauce turned me into a baby, maybe it'll turn her into a baby. I was about to make a grab for it, but Grandma Esther grabbed me.

She pinned me up against the refrigerator, causing it to shake.

"How I want you, Baby Jackie! Baby Jackie! Baby Jackie! Baby Jackie!" She began to chant.

She put her hands around my throat and squeezed.

"Baby Jackie! Baby Jackie! BABY JACKIE!" I managed to grab the applesauce with my left hand. Then, I threw the entire bowl of applesauce at Grandma Esther. It splashed all over her face and housedress.

Slowly, she backed up away from me. Grandma Esther twitched violently. She started to shrink...shrink until all of her clothes fell off of her body. Sitting on the floor was baby Grandma Esther. She started wailing and crying.

"How do you like that? I did it!" Grandma Esther had gotten a taste of her own medicine. She continued crying and crying. I took her upstairs and put her in the crib.

Later, I cleaned myself up and packed my bag to go home. Mom came over, and she held her arms out to give me a hug.

"I've missed you so much," she gushed. We hugged for what felt like forever.

"Missed you too." We let go of our hug.

"Hey, where's Grandma Esther. I want to thank her for taking care of you."

"Well—" I paused when I heard Grandma Esther crying upstairs.

"Who's that crying?" Mom asked.

"I think Grandma is busy right now. We should go."

I shoved her toward the door, and we left the house.

The next day, I came back to Grandma Esther's house. I ran upstairs and into the guest room. Baby Grandma Esther was in the crib, with tears in her eyes and a pout on her face, as if to

make me feel guilty for what I did to her. After all, she was still my Grandma. I wasn't going to abandon her the way Mom did it.

"I'll feed you something," I said, picking her up out of the crib.

I did feel a *little* guilty for turning her into a baby. The least I can do is take care of her each day after school. I came into the kitchen and set Baby Grandma Esther into the high chair. I went into the cabinet and took out a can of creamed sweet potatoes. Then, I opened the jar and scooped a spoonful of it, and held it out in front of her.

"Eat up Grandma, It's your favorite. Eat. Eat."

HAUNTED HOUSE VIDEO

There were many cool and weird things one could find on the web. Damian loved to surf the web. His parents had gone out for date night. As Damion continued to surf, a pop-up came on his screen. The pop-up read, Dr. Creeps Horror Videos. Interested, Damion clicked on it. The pop-up led him to a black screen that seemed to take forever to load.

"Come on, load!" he said impatiently, pulling his black hair. Finally, there was a shot of someone's front porch. The camera was focused on the front door. The person recording didn't show their face. The camera moved toward the door. The individual knocked on it several times. Suddenly, Damion heard knocking on his front door. He paused the video and went downstairs.

He opened the front door, but nobody was there. *Hmmm. That's weird.* Damion thought. He shrugged it off and closed the door. It could be some kids just messing with me. Damion decided. He went back upstairs and played the video again. The unknown person let out a chuckle. It sounded like a man. The man moved away from the porch and started walking toward the side door. Using great force, He knocked on the door.. A few seconds later, Damion heard someone knocking on the side door.

I'll catch those stupid kids this time. he thought. He paused the video and went downstairs to the side door.

Damion opened up his side door. There was no one! He looked out onto the sidewalk. He didn't see or hear anyone running away. *Weird.* Damion thought. He went back inside and watched the video again. The individual waited at the side door for a few seconds. Then, the person sprinted in the backyard, shaking the camera furiously.

He walked over to a large door which was a walk-out basement. The man used a crowbar to smash on the door until it broke. He walked down the stairs and started running through the basement. At that moment, Damion heard noises coming from *his* basement. There was no way that children were down there. Damion paused the video and stood at the doorway.

He imagined creepy things down there. But he had to toughen up and see what was going on. Nervously, he walked down one step at a time. Cautiously, he stared down into the dark basement. His brown eyes widened in fear. No one there. Not a soul.

What's going on here? Damion thought. *Is someone breaking in or what?* Quickly, he ran out of the basement and back upstairs to his room. Being extra careful, he locked the bedroom. He couldn't call the police or tell them about the supposed intruder because he had no concrete proof.

Damion calmed down and watched the video again. The man was still down in the basement. He walked up the creaky steps into the living room. The living room looked very similar to Damion's. Immediately, the person walked past the living room and up the stairs. As Damion watched, he heard someone booming up his stairs!

Oh my god! It's the video! The man is in my house! He thought. In the video, the man stopped in front of the bedroom door. He jiggled on the doorknob. Suddenly, Damion's doorknob began to jiggle too.

The man is at my door. He looked around the room for a weapon. He rummaged under his bed. Nothing. He looked in his closet. Nothing. Absolutely nothing that would work.

In the video, the man started hitting the bedroom door with his crowbar. BANG. BANG. The man stopped. There was an eerie silence now. Damion stood frozen, shaking in fear. Suddenly, the man dressed in all black, wearing a clown mask, kicked in the door with a crowbar in his hand. Damion screamed and screamed for bloody life. The man walked closer. He stood an inch in front of Damion. He removed his mask, revealing a middle-aged face with gray-stubble and piercing blue eyes.

"Who the hell are you? What are you gonna do?" Damion asked.

"You must be eliminated."

The man raised the crowbar and stabbed it right through Damion's face. Blood spurted on his bed, the hardwood floor and on the man's black clothing. The man took his long slender finger and stuck it in the pool of blood on the floor. He held up his finger and licked the blood right off.

"Delicious."

* * *

Click.

"Stupid movie!" Eric yelled. He and his friend Martha had just finished watching *The Haunted House* video.

"It was good," Martha gushed.

"The ending was lame."

THE STRANGE SCHOOL

Before Mark Ackerman went to Green Valley Boarding School, he was considered a problem-child. It wasn't his idea to go. This all started because of his mother. Three days ago, Mark Ackerman drove home after being expelled from his fifth public school that year. He heard his mother crying in the kitchen.

"Mom, I'm home!"

Mark entered the kitchen where he saw his mother with her head down on the kitchen table, sobbing. She raised her head up and stared at him with her eyes red from crying.

"Y-y-your principal called me, you got ex-expelled," Mrs. Ackerman said through choked sobs, "W-why would you get those two innocent girls pregnant? Y-you ruined their lives. N-now you got them kicked out of school too."

"Those sluts deserved it," Mark said, "They were desperate and needed some fucking male attention. Then, they have the audacity to get mad when they receive it."

Mrs. Ackerman wiped tears from her face with her hand.

"I honestly don't know what to do with you," she whimpered, "I f-failed as a parent. Not only this but your grades have been terrible. This has gone on far enough. This is the last straw."

"Boo-hoo, cut the tears and make me something to eat."

Mrs. Ackerman sat up from the table and went over to the kitchen counter. She picked up something and showed it to Mark. It was a brochure for a school. On the front, it read:

**Come down to Green Valley Boarding school!
It's a 3-week program guaranteed to turn your
terrible boys into respectable young men!**

There were photos of the large campus with many buildings. Also, there were pictures of teen boys smiling and giving thumbs up.

"I didn't want to tell you this but…I've enrolled you into this program. You start tomorrow and I advise you to start packing now." Mrs. Ackerman said.

"WHAT! No! No! I can't go here! This school looks lame! I don't need it!" Mark protested.

"Sorry Mark, but it's for your own good. This school has a 100 percent success rate in changing troublemakers. After this program, things are gonna be different around here. Now go upstairs now!"

Mark kicked the wall and stomped toward the stairs.

Things are gonna be different, she says. Not if I can help it. Mark thought.

* * *

The next morning, Mark and his mother stood outside on the front lawn, waiting for the Green Valley bus.

"You're the worst mother ever. You know that right?" Mark said.

"I'm gonna be glad you get sent away. Even for two weeks. It's gonna be like heaven," Mrs. Ackerman shot back, "So help me, that I try to help my troubled son." Mark saw the yellow school bus from around the corner and drive down his street. The bus stopped directly in front of their house. A chubby-bus driver with tufts of black hair stepped out and grabbed Mark's suitcases and put them in the back.

"Good luck Mark. I hope you learn something from this experience," Mrs. Ackerman said.

Mark rolled his eyes and got on the bus. The driver got back into his seat. Mrs. Ackerman gave Mark a final wave before the doors closed. Mark looked and saw the bus was practically empty except for one boy in the middle row. The boy had jet black hair that was unkempt along with huge brown eyes. His eyes sort of lit up when he saw Mark.

Mark sat next to him and the bus sped off.

"Looks like we're the newcomers since we're the only ones on the bus," the boy said, "I'm Jaden."

"Mark," Mark responded quickly as he took out his earbuds and placed them in his ears.

"You have a nice house. I saw it," Jaden said.

"Thanks…I guess," Mark responded.

"Is the Range Rover that was in your driveway, yours? It's nice."

"Yeah, it's mine, duh."

Why is this dude trying to talk to me? Can't he see I have my earbuds in? Mark thought.

"Your mother is very hot," Jaden said, "You seem to have it all. Hot mother, nice car, nice house. Everything. I live in Penngrove which you know is a shitty town. It's dirt poor. I don't even live in a house but more like a dusty ass shack."

"Sucks to be you," Mark said.

I'm gonna hurt this loser if he doesn't shut up. After that, Jaden didn't talk to Mark for the rest of the ride. The bus eventually pulled up to the large school. There was a sign greeting them that said: WELCOME TO GREEN VALLEY. They saw a huge campus with two tall

buildings connected to each other. A sign on top of the left building read: SCHOOL. The

building on the right had many windows and was about five stories high. The top of that building

read: DORMITORY.

The bus stopped in front of the dormitory. A red-faced man stepped out of the building.

He had black hair that was beginning to gray. The man also had a perfect gray stubble that really

complimented his hair. He also wore an all-blue school uniform with a handgun holster strapped

to his left pant leg, like a police officer. Mark knew this person meant business.

"Off the bus!" the bus driver gruffed. Jaden and Mark got off the bus and the bus driver unloaded their stuff. He took out all of our things and we stood in front of the man.

"You two must be the newcomers. I'm Dean Mathis, the head of this school," the grumpy man said, "You were sent here to shape up and toughen up. I know you can't do that on your own because you're too lazy and ignorant to follow any directions."

Lazy? Who was this guy to call us lazy? How the fuck can he know we're lazy? Mark thought.

"Umm, I'm not lazy," Mark spoke up.

Jaden turned and looked at Mark. Dean Mathis stood there, face turning even redder,

and his fists clenched. Slowly, he walked up to him and asked, "What's your name, maggot?"

"Mark, Mark Ackerman."

He could see his face getting even redder, it was as red as a watermelon.

"You may want to chill out, tiger. You don't want to explode," Mark remarked. Suddenly,

Dean Mathis grabbed his shoulders.

"Listen here, maggot. I've got my eye on you. Any more funny business…well… who knows what's gonna happen to you."

"You don't scare me."

"Once you start, you'll wish you've never said that," Dean Mathis said.

Then, two men came up behind Dean Mathis. They looked like bodyguards. They wore

blue uniforms and had big bulging muscles. One of them wore an earring in his left ear The other had a large snake tattoo on his right arm.

"Take them up to their dorms," Dean Mathis ordered them.

"Follow us," Left Earring said in a deep husky voice. The boys followed him inside the

building. There was a large lobby with couches and a large chandelier. At the end of the lobby was a lit hallway. They came closer and saw many doors labeled with all the names of students in alphabetical order by last name. Mark saw his name on the tag read:

Ackerman, Mark

"You have five minutes to settle in! Your school uniforms will be sitting on your beds!

You must put them on!" Left Earring shouted. Mark covered his ears. *That dude sure shouts a lot.* he thought. He opened up the door. It was unlocked surprisingly. Inside the room, Mark saw a button next to the door. He pushed it and heard a click on the door. Mark jiggled the doorknob, it was locked. *Hmm, odd way of locking a door.* He checked out the room. There was a bed, a sofa, a dresser, and a small seating area. On the bed, sat my school uniform. It was the same blue school uniform Dean Mathis had on along with tan slacks and black dress shoes.

"Home sweet home for the year," Mark groaned unhappily. He went into the bathroom and put his school uniform on. The pants were too tight and the shirt was a size too big for him.

This is gonna be a very long two weeks. Mark thought.

* * *

Mark and Jaden both were taken to a classroom in the school building. The teacher wasn't there yet and everyone in the class was chatting noisily. Some were checking out Mark and Jaden. Presumably, because they were new.

Just then, a man walked into the classroom along with three other boys. The three boys work the same blue uniform and slacks as the rest of the class. Except they wore white ribbons on their uniform.

Must be graduates. Mark thought.

Their expressions were blank and their eyes were wide. The man looked like he came out of the military. He had a blond buzz cut along with a beefy red face as red as a watermelon. He was as skinny as a toothpick and wore a blue school uniform along with matching blue loafers. The man held a stack of packets in his hand.

"We have new students," he said in a husky voice, while looking at Mark and Jaden sitting in the back. "I'm, Mr. Patterson."

This guy looks like fun. Mark rolled his eyes.

"These are our new graduates," Mr. Patterson said, pointing at the kids, "Would you three care to demonstrate how good you've become?"

"Yes sir," the boy in the middle of the three said.

"Alright, can you three please take a seat?"

The three boys simultaneously walked over to three seats in the front. At the exact same time, each boy sat down. They said nothing. They had blank expressions.

"Ok, now march one lap around this classroom," Mr. Patterson ordered.

Each boy shot up at the same time and they began to march. As they marched, they each held out their left hand. Then, they held out their right. The boys were even moving on the same *foot* as each other. Moving at the same rhythm. Left, right, left, right.

They're like little robots. Mark thought.

The boys finished the lap and they walked up and each shook Mr. Patterson's hand.

"It was nice having you," Mr. Patterson said.

"It was a pleasure," one of the boys said. Then they left.

"That's what I want you guys to be like at the end of this program. So obedient. Such enthusiasm to follow instructions. Such good manners." Mr. Patterson said. He began to hand out the packets. He handed Mark one.

Ugh, a test? Really, on the first day? I'm not good at taking tests. Mark thought. He opened the packet and looked at the questions. They were standard questions at first. They were asking for birth date, name, city, and age. But as Mark scanned the packet further, some of the questions were a little too weird. One question asked, What do you call your parents? Another asked, What's your first memory? Mark frantically ripped through the pages. There were pages after pages of such disturbing and weird questions.

Why do they need to know this? Why is this important? he thought.

"Hey, aren't these questions weird?" Jaden whispered to Mark.

"Hell yes, what kind of test is this?"

"NO TALKING!" Mr. Patterson yelled.

"Why does the school need to know these things?" Jaden asked.

"I dunno," Mark thought.

"ACKERMAN! GO TO THE DEAN'S OFFICE!" Mr. Patterson boomed as he pointed to the door.

Mark sat up and walked out the door and headed to Dean Mathis's office. Once he got there, Dean Mathis stood at the doorway as if he were expecting him.

"I knew you'd be a tough case," he said, glaring at Mark, "Your program will be accelerated. Your ritual is now in five days."

He let out a sigh and then said, "Now go back up to your room and don't come out until dinner. I shall figure out your punishment tomorrow morning."

Dean Mathis shooed Mark away and he left.

Why was I singled out? Jaden was talking too. Mark thought. He sighed and went back to his room. *I already hate it here. These teachers are so rude.* As Mark walked outside back to the dormitory building. He knew he had a plan. He had to call his mother and tell her to come to get him. He had to make up a story as to why he had to leave.

I need my cellphone. Those guards confiscated our phones. Mark thought bitterly. He walked inside the dormitory building with a big smile on his face. He knew he was home free.

Dinner time came and everyone sat in the cafeteria. Mark knew his plan to call his mother was to sneak out during this time. The meal was horrendous. It was some dry and gray meatloaf with clumpy mash potatoes that tasted like chalk.

"This meal is awful, don't you hate this?" Jaden asked, "It's like fucking prison."

"I really don't care about that. I'm trying to go home." Mark said.

"How?"

"I have to call my mom."

Mark looked toward the cafeteria exit and saw Snake Tattoo and Left Earring guarding it. He had a plan though. Mark got up and walked over to them.

"What do you want, maggot?" Left Earring growled.

"I need to use the bathroom," Mark said.

"Make it quick."

Mark rushed past them and came out into the hallway. He started down the hallway and headed up the staircase at the end. He got to the second floor and ran down to the office at the end of the hall. The office door was left wide open. Mark peeked inside, it was empty.

Sweet. he thought. He rushed inside the office and gazed around. It was a large office with a huge bay window looking outside in the center along with a wooden desk there too. To the left of the desk were a bunch of file cabinets. On top of them, he saw the blue bin where the phones were confiscated.

Mark set the bin on the desk and opened it. He rummaged inside for his phone until he found it at the bottom of the pile. Quickly, he dialed his mother's number and it rang. Mrs. Ackerman picked up on the third ring with a tired, "Mark, why are you calling me now?"

"Mom! You have to get me out of here!"

"Mark, why are you calling me now? What are you up to?"

"No! Listen! This school is horrible. The teachers are mean, the food is terrible, and there was this weird test today with these strange questions. This school is strange!"

"I see you're not changing at all, Mark." Mrs. Ackerman said, "You're only making this harder on yourself."

"B-but–" Before Mark could say another word, the phone was snatched from his hand. Mark looked and saw Dean Mathis glaring at him. He didn't hear him come inside the office at all. Dean Mathis brought the phone to his ear.

"Hi, is this Mark's mother?" Dean Mathis said, "Yes, this is Dean Mathis, the head of this school. I'm so sorry that your son called you with all these crazy trivialities. He's been a bit of a troublemaker so far but we're going to work him out for you."

Mrs. Ackerman said something else Mark couldn't hear.

"He's being sent home early. He'll be ready in two days. Mark's a very special boy."

They continued talking.

"Okay, bye," Dean Mathis said and he hung up the phone. He returned his glare back to Mark.

"Three times in one day. What a shame. Some kids just never learn." Dean Mathis said, shaking his head, "Your program will be accelerated once more. Your ritual is in two days. Now get out of here."

Mark left the office in a hurry. Ritual. *What does he mean by ritual? What's going to happen in two days? What's going on in this school?* Mark continued back to the cafeteria for dessert. *Why was my program cut? Are they going to send me home early, the same way I walked in? Why would he do that?* Mark sighed. He had too many questions.

* * *

That night, Mark laid in bed, trying to sleep. The mattress was hard as a rock. It was already making Mark's back sore. When he was finally about to doze off, Mark heard a big bloodcurdling scream.

"YAIIIIIIIIIIIIIIIIIIIIIIIIIIIIIIIIIIIIIIIIIIIIIIIIIII!"

"YAIIIIIIIIIIIIIIIIIIIIIIIIIIIIIIIIIIIIIIIIIIIIIIIIIII!"

It rang throughout the room. Mark shot up, wide-eyed. Then, he heard the scream again.

"YAIIIIIIIIIIIIIIIIIIIIIIIIIIIIIIIIIIIIIIIIIIIIIIIIIII!"

It sounded like a boy's scream. *But where is it coming from.* Mark wondered.

"YAIIIIIIIIIIIIIIIIIIIIIIIIIIIIIIIIIIIIIIIIIIIIIIIIIII!"

The scream seemed close. Mark put his pillow over his face and tried to go back to sleep. But the screaming wouldn't get out of his head.

* * *

"Can I help you clean?" Jaden asked, reaching for the mop.

"I don't care," Mark said. They were in the cafeteria the next morning. Mark's punishment for his trouble-making was to clean the entire cafeteria. Mark hated cleaning. He found it gross.

"Has this school ever heard of a fucking janitor?" Mark asked as he wiped down a table, furiously. That's when he remembered the screams from last night. He wondered if Jaden had heard them too.

"Hey Jaden, did you hear any screaming last night?" Jaden stopped mopping and looked at Mark, bewildered. "Huh?"

"Did you hear screams last night?"

"Um, no. I didn't hear screams coming from the school. I slept like a log."

"Hmmm, that's weird."

Those screams were pretty loud. How did Jaden or anyone not hear them? What's going on? Mark continued to spray down the tables and wipe them. Still puzzled. *There is definitely something this school is hiding. Something terrible. I can't stick around and find out. I have to get out of here ASAP.*

* * *

During lunch, Mark was in Mr. Patterson's class. He had to complete the packet that he neglected to do. Mr. Patterson wouldn't let him leave until it was done. Reluctantly, Mark had to answer all the questions. He finished in less than twenty minutes. Mark brought up the packet to Mr. Patterson's desk.

"Done already?" Mr. Patterson asked. He scanned through the packet and then set it down. Mark left the classroom and started toward the cafeteria. That's when he heard the scream come from somewhere behind him.

"YAIIIIIIIIIIIIIIII!"

Startled, Mark ran back into the direction he came.

"LET ME GO! LET ME GO! DON'T DO THIS TO ME!" He heard a boy's voice yell. Mark ran down the hallway, sprinting past empty classrooms until he reached the end and there were two more hallways going off to the left and right. They

"LET ME GO! LET ME GO!"

Mark heard the screams coming from the right. He turned the right corner and then quietly. He saw Dean Mathis, Snake Tattoo, and Left Earring. Snake Tattoo held a boy over his shoulders. Mark could see the boy's terrified face. Dean Mathis knocked on a tile on the floor. Then the tile began to slide, revealing an opening inside. Mark gasped.

"We're already for the ritual. We shall make you a respectable young man. All of your evil sins will be gone." Dean Mathis said, "Years of disobedience and trouble-making shall come to an end."

The four of them disappeared inside the tile, down what looked like a stairway. The tile slid close after them. Immediately, Mark ran away. He stampeded down the hallways and eventually past the cafeteria. Mark didn't feel like eating. He wanted to get to his room.

Oh my goodness. There is something going on here! I think they're going to mind-control that boy into being good. My ritual is tomorrow! I have to get out of here tonight. Mark thought. He made it back to his room and sat on the bed. He knew he had to escape.

I need a plan. I have to escape tonight. Mark sat on the bed, twiddling his thumbs until a plan lit up in his head. That's when he smiled. He knew what he had to do.

* * *

At 10:00 every night, it was lights-out. Everyone had to be in bed. But Mark wasn't going to bed. At 9:58, he sat on top of his bed, fully clothed, with the light off. Waiting for 10:00. Snake Tattoo and Left Earring would do their rounds up and down the hallway to make sure all the lights were out. At 10:00 sharp, that's when Mark heard the guards leave the hallway and disappear out of the building.

It's time. Mark thought. He sat up out of bed and went to the first-story window. Quietly, he unlatched the window and flung it open. A whoosh of cold air filled the room. Mark crawled out of the window and dropped onto the grass. He shut the window behind him. Mark began to stride across the campus. There were flood lights, lighting up the campus. In the distance, Mark saw Snake Tattoo and Left Earring, guarding the school building.

Damn, if I run into the lights, they'll definitely see me. Mark thought. He scanned the area until he saw some bushes under the flood lights. Gingerly, Mark stepped behind a bush and ducked down. Slowly, he crawled on the grass, going behind each bush. The bushes ended and Mark sat up. He looked back and saw that Snake Tattoo and Left Earring were still standing there. He was further away from them.

That's when Mark began to speed-walk past the buildings and into the parking lot. He began to run through the parking lot but was stopped by a fence. There was a tall barbed-wire fence, blocking his escape. It was about twenty-four feet tall.

Damn, what now? Mark thought. A dead end. From behind, a hand grabbed his shoulder, causing Mark to shriek.

"YAAAA!" Mark turned around and saw Jaden standing behind him.

"Oh thank goodness, it's you," he said, letting out a sigh of relief, "You have to help me escape. So–"

"I know a better place to go. Follow me." Jaden said. Mark followed Jaden and they turned away from the fence. Walked through the parking lot and they were back on the campus.

"Jaden, why are we going back to the campus?" Mark asked, "The guards will see us."

Jaden stopped in his tracks and looked back at Mark. A glare was now on his face.

"Oh Mark, you're not going anywhere. Except going back down to the dungeon for your ritual."

"What? Jaden, what are you talking about?"

Jaden chuckled, "I'm working for Dean Mathis. You see, every kid that comes to this program has to go through the ritual to turn them into goody-two-shoes. But you have to die. I want your life."

"What? No! No!"

"How do you think parents find out about this place? Well, I'm the one who sends the brochures. To nudge their parents to send their terrible kids here. I spy on all the bad kids in this state. Until I saw you, I've been watching you for a while. At your school. I know you got those girls pregnant. That's when I saw your perfect house, your perfect mother, and your perfect car."

Jaden paused. "I want it all! I want all of your life! I have no family! I'm just a robotic shapeshifter, created by Dean Mathis. I crave a normal life. In exchange, for that, I have to kill you. That was the deal, Dean Mathis and I made."

Jaden pulled out a pocket knife and began to stagger over to Mark.

"Sorry, I have to do this," he said, his expression blank.

"NO!" Mark yelled. Jaden raised the knife and went for a stab.

* * *

"Mark has really learned something from this program! Isn't this exciting, Dave? The beginning of a new era," Mrs. Ackerman said at dinner.

"It sure is!" Mr. Ackerman said, putting his last forkful of spaghetti in his mouth, "Proud of my boy."

"Will you please clear the plates, Mark?" Mrs. Ackerman asked.

"Yes mam," Mark said. He got up and cleared everyone's plates, then washed the dishes. Then, he went upstairs to his room. He felt a little terrible for killing Jaden. Well, Jaden was trying to kill him first but he missed. Then, Mark took the knife from him, killing Jaden. He went back to Dean Mathis, pretending to be Jaden, also telling him that he succeeded. Then Dean Mathis sent him back home. Not knowing that he wasn't Jaden, pretending to be him.

He was still the terrible boy he always was.

I just have to pretend to be good for the rest of my life. They'll never know, I'm faking. I'm too good. I always have tricks up my sleeve.